Dear Rea

Welcome

Though I know an actual Buckhorn exists, mine is an entirely fictional town in beautiful Kentucky. My first Buckhorn story was published back in 2000 and the series has become a true reader favorite. For me it seemed a natural fit to combine my need to help stray cats and dogs by continuing the series with a new generation of the leading family in Buckhorn.

Through a special contract with my publisher, the advance and all royalties on *A Buckhorn Baby* will go directly to the Animal Adoption Foundation, a local no-kill animal shelter that does an amazing job healing, protecting, and loving cats and dogs until a "forever home" can be found for them.

I hope you enjoy Amber and Noel's long-awaited story, and I especially hope you enjoy knowing that by purchasing this story, you've helped a dog or cat in need. And don't miss *A Buckhorn Bachelor*, my 2016 benefit novella, included as a bonus in this collection!

To see other "benefit books," visit http://lorifoster.com/benefit-books/

And to see other books in the Buckhorn series, visit http://lorifoster.com/connected-books/#buckhorn

From the bottom of my heart, thank you!

Lori Foster

Also available from Lori Foster and HQN Books

Body Armor

Under Pressure
Hard Justice

Guthrie Brothers

Don't Tempt Me

An Ultimate Novel

Hard Knocks
(prequel ebook novella)
No Limits
Holding Strong
Tough Love
Fighting Dirty

Love Undercover

Run the Risk
Bare It All
Getting Rowdy
Dash of Peril

Edge of Honor

Ready, Set, Jett
(ebook novella)
When You Dare
Trace of Fever
Savor the Danger
A Perfect Storm
What Chris Wants
(ebook novella)

Other must-reads

A Buckhorn Baby
Built for Love
(ebook novella)
A Buckhorn Bachelor
(ebook novella)
A Buckhorn Summer
(ebook novella)
All For You
Back to Buckhorn
(ebook novella)
Heartbreakers
Charade
Up in Flames
Turn Up the Heat
Hot in Here
Animal Attraction
(ebook anthology)
Love Bites
All Riled Up
The Buckhorn Legacy
Forever Buckhorn
Buckhorn Beginnings
Bewitched
Unbelievable
Tempted
Bodyguard
Caught!
Fallen Angels
Enticing

Look for the next sizzling Guthrie Brothers book

Worth the Wait

LORI FOSTER

A BUCKHORN BABY

Margie,
All my best,
Lori Foster

HQN™

HQN™

Recycling programs for this product may not exist in your area.

ISBN-13: 978-1-488-03041-3

A Buckhorn Baby & A Buckhorn Bachelor

This edition published by arrangement with Harlequin Books S.A.

For questions and comments about the quality of this book, please contact us at CustomerService@Harlequin.com.

www.HQNBooks.com

Printed in U.S.A.

CONTENTS

A BUCKHORN BABY

CHAPTER ONE

BRIGHT SUNSHINE DANCED through the leaves of towering elms and oaks, adding dappled shade to the gathering of family. They sat at multiple picnic tables and in lawn chairs scattered about. Many of her cousins had brought their dogs to play with her father's and uncle's animals. For once, Amber Hudson hadn't brought along her own fur-baby, Rookie. They'd spent the morning together, taken a walk, played fetch in the yard, and then she'd left him in the fenced-in backyard, but with the doggy door open so he could come and go in the house as he pleased.

Their group had grown, she thought with a smile, seeing the spouses of her brother and cousins, who were now a part of it all. Everyone joined in for Father's Day since they had some of the best dads ever.

Filled with love and pride and warm affection, she smiled at her own father. Morgan Hudson was an amazing icon in the community; she wasn't the only one who adored him. Everyone in Buckhorn, Kentucky, cared for her dad.

He'd be so surprised by her announcement, and no doubt her uncles would cheer right along with everyone else.

Her family, more than most, loved babies.

Her gaze skipped over to Noel Poet, the reason she

hadn't brought Rookie along. She hoped to visit with Noel directly after the gathering—and by *visit*, she meant touch all over, maybe kiss all over, and explore again that off-the-charts sexual chemistry. More and more each day, she craved him whenever they were apart.

Considering the night he'd had, it amazed her that he'd made it today. As usual, her heart skipped a beat at the sight of him. Thanks to the current heat and humidity, sweat darkened the ends of his blond hair. He wore loose board shorts that showed off his hairy calves, laceless sneakers on his big feet and a T-shirt printed with STILL PLAYS WITH FIRETRUCKS.

Fighting exhaustion, he slouched against a tree, using one thick shoulder as a prop to keep him on his feet as he spoke to her mother, Misty.

Because of a barn fire the night before, he couldn't have gotten much rest. Noel wouldn't complain, though. He never did. It went against his man-code, which had helped solidify his friendship with the men in her family, since they were all a bunch of "suffer in silence"-type guys, too.

Continually Noel's dark brown eyes sought her out with a sort of casual possessiveness that thrilled her.

Noel was quiet and contained, strong and heroic, with a rock-hard body, a gorgeous, expressive face, and Lord help her, she had it bad for him. Of course, she hadn't told him that, because he hadn't yet told her. She'd tried every trick in the book to get him to open up on how he felt, but other than presenting himself as her steady date and showing a lot of sexual compatibility, he kept his thoughts to himself.

Her father liked Noel. Her mother adored him. Her cousins all respected him.

Amber frowned as she considered things. Around Noel, she didn't feel like her usual cocky, take-charge self. Somehow he made her feel…more feminine. Even delicate.

She snorted at that nonsense.

Her daddy hadn't raised any wimps, never mind how he'd always pampered her.

She and Noel were more on than off, so why did she lose her edge around him?

When Noel laughed, she sighed in confused longing—until Garrett nudged her.

"Plotting his capture?" her brother asked.

Startled, Amber frowned up at him, opened her mouth, drew a blank on anything witty and said only "Shut up."

Garrett's brows climbed high. "That's it? That's your comeback?"

Lifting her long, loose braid away from her neck, she grumbled a low, indistinct curse.

Garrett whistled. "He must really have you running in circles, sis, because you're way off your game."

True. When it came to Noel, she had no game at all. She'd matched up numerous people in Buckhorn, Kentucky, using a knack for machination. But Noel often distracted her enough that she couldn't think, much less plot.

Around him, all she could do was *feel.*

Taking in her expression, Garrett drew her close, kissed her forehead and asked, "Want me to stomp on him?"

"Ha." It wouldn't be easy to do, given Noel and her

brother were equally buff and bullheaded. But that wasn't the point. "Touch him and you answer to me."

Garrett's smile came slowly. "That's more like it. Just remember, if necessary, I got your back."

"He works for you, Garrett."

Her brother ran the fire station, and Noel was the newest firefighter under his command. More important than that, they were friends.

"So?" Garrett said, discounting it all. "You're my sister. That trumps everything else." Leaving her to think on that, Garrett headed to his wife. Zoey wore a yellow sundress, her feet bare in the lush grass. She had her brown hair in a high ponytail and a permanent smile on her mouth. After Garrett lifted her high, then kissed her soundly, she looked positively radiant.

Before the two of them could sneak off, Amber quit mooning over Noel and instead climbed up to stand on a picnic-table seat. "Attention, please. I have an announcement to make!"

Slowly the din of conversation faded and everyone faced her. Remaining up on the bench and lacing her fingers together, Amber said, "I'm so glad everyone made it at the same time this year, because I have something very special to share."

Almost as one, heads swiveled to look at Noel in expectation.

Oops, Amber thought. She hadn't meant to give the impression that her announcement had to do with Noel. Of course, that was the obvious assumption…except that Noel hadn't declared himself. Not even close.

Before he could propose, he'd need to tell her that he loved her. Hopefully soon.

With her entire family scrutinizing him, Noel briefly

closed his eyes, blew out a breath and, ignoring everyone else, returned his attention to Amber with exaggerated patience.

Others took the hint and followed suit.

Barely keeping her happiness contained, Amber said, "Since it's Father's Day, this is especially for you, Dad."

Morgan Hudson sat a little straighter, and again, his gaze cut to Noel. Her mother nudged him, not that it did much good.

Well used to the teasing of her family, Amber only smiled and then announced, "Dad, you're going to be a grandpa."

Several things happened at once.

Noel lost his balance against the tree and hit the ground. Hard.

Morgan Hudson's chair toppled as he shot to his feet.

And Garrett yelled, "It's Zoey and me!" Then with a wide grin, he added, "We're going to have a baby."

NOEL WAS STILL RATTLED.

Good God Almighty, Amber had taken a year off his life. She could have been a little more straightforward in the way she'd handled that whole thing. It didn't surprise him that Amber was the one to make the announcement. In most things, her entire family allowed her to take the lead, and no doubt Garrett and Zoey were happy to let her present the news.

She did so with flair.

But for a flash of an instant, he'd thought the entire family would turn on him, with Morgan Hudson leading the charge.

It didn't help that her family was so large, so vocal and so protective. Good thing Garrett had interpreted the misunderstanding right off and was more direct than Amber when he shouted the correction.

And why, now that her family knew the truth, did they continue to cast suspicious looks his way? They should know him well enough by now to know he wouldn't be bullied into doing or saying anything until he was ready to do so.

"Need a drink?"

He glanced behind him and found Lisa, Amber's cousin who'd recently married Gray Neely, offering him a frosty Coke.

"Sure, thanks." After Amber's little stunt, it wasn't the type of drink he needed, but at least Lisa looked as open and friendly as ever. "The heat is a killer today."

After falling, he'd stayed down and now only propped his back against the tree.

Lisa sat opposite him on the grass, her feet tucked to the side of her. Trying not to smile, she asked, "You okay?"

"What? Oh, yeah. I'm fine. Late night, that's all. The fire—"

"I meant that mild heart attack you had at the mention of a baby."

Noel choked on his cola.

Rising to her knees, Lisa thwacked him on the back. "You did realize right off that she was talking about a baby, right?"

Yeah, he'd known—and he really wished everyone would quit throwing around that word. He wanted no part of it, not in conversation, not in reality. He coughed several times, cleared his throat and nodded.

"Such a reaction," Adam said, coming up to join his sister...and heckle Noel.

"Not enough sleep," Noel explained again, hoping that lame excuse would suffice. Just as Adam sat, Noel pushed to his feet. "In fact, I think I'll—"

He turned to flee and almost ran into Amber.

She stood there, hands on her slim hips, that dark, thick braid over her shoulder, curved around one lush breast. Her beautiful blue eyes dared him.

Noel couldn't help but grin. No one affected him the way Amber did. She left him in a heightened state of sexual awareness—and he liked it. Her ballsy attitude, as much as her sensual appearance, appealed to him. For such a slender, feminine woman, she had the air of an Amazon.

Amber cast a warning glace at her cousins, and they wisely departed, grins in place. Plastering on her own smile, she turned to Noel and, sounding uncharacteristically shy, said, "Hey."

Mixed emotions kept him mum. That timidity didn't suit her at all and told him she was about to go beyond her comfort zone. Probably all the blasted talk about babies.

He thought about making his excuses and removing himself from range, but he happened to look at her mouth, and the familiar urge to kiss her overrode everything else.

Murmuring, "Hey yourself," he leaned forward and brushed his mouth over those soft, full lips he adored. He meant to keep it light, but her lips parted, which invited his to press more firmly, and suddenly he was lost to a full-blown, tongue-twining, hot and wet mating of the mouths.

Amber had snaked her slim arms around his neck. He mindlessly drew her closer to his body.

A deep breath filled his head with her heated scent and he shifted to her neck, tasting her velvety skin, quickly losing control.

Head back and eyes closed, she whispered, "Were you leaving?"

Reality slammed him back into the here and now.

He had been about to go, yeah, but now he shook his head. "Just trying to escape your family." His hands rested on the top of her shapely hips. Amber was warm, soft, and her irresistible scent teased him.

If they were alone, he'd free her from that body-hugging tank top so he could get to her full breasts...

Rather than take it as a joke, the way he meant it, she softly chided him. "Don't let them scare you off."

So she'd seen the truth? Of course she had. Being far too perceptive, Amber often recognized things in people, things that others missed.

"It hasn't happened yet," he reminded her. But yeah, today the dynamic seemed to have taken a drastic shift.

Amber came from a family of overachievers, community leaders and really, really good people. From reputations alone, they could intimidate others. But meeting them in person, getting to know them, really sealed the deal. Her family was nothing short of amazing.

Her dad, especially, was impressive, not only in size—because Morgan Hudson was a man who, even in his early sixties, remained strong as an ox—but also as an icon who'd fulfilled the role of sheriff and now mayor. He was involved in just about every community program that existed in Buckhorn.

Hell, he ran most of them, fulfilling his main need to

help those less fortunate and his equally obvious need to control his small corner of the world.

Noel didn't want to be controlled. He'd had his hands full fending off Amber's tendency to take charge. She, like her father, had a very strong will. But deep down, he knew Amber hadn't gotten seriously involved with anyone, despite being a beautiful, smart, independent woman, because she hadn't yet met her match.

He matched her, in nearly every way. Together they were combustible.

She stared up at him with those amazing incandescent blue eyes framed by thick black lashes. Her eyes were the feature that had first caught his attention, closely followed by her sweet body, and then her bold persona had finished him off. She epitomized a temptation trifecta and he couldn't resist.

"Noel?" Her tongue licked nervously at her bottom lip.

Noel's blood fired. Wanting to be alone with her, he glanced around, hoping for inspiration—and caught the smirking gaze of her brother and the "dare you to" stare of her father.

Well, hell.

"We're drawing attention," he told her and defiantly hugged her a little closer. At twenty-seven, Amber didn't need anyone's permission to be with him. And at thirty, he sure as hell didn't ask for it, not even from the reigning family of the town.

Her gaze warmed. "Want to go swimming?"

"Where?" If she meant off the dock with everyone else, he'd have to pass. His reaction to Amber in a bikini wasn't conducive to an audience.

She trailed a finger down his chest. "How about—"

"Amber, honey, would you mind helping me in the kitchen?" Misty Hudson, her mother, smiled sweetly at each of them.

Innate good manners came forward. It was one thing to ignore the men in her family, quite another to be that rude to her mother. Noel released Amber and stepped back respectfully.

"Mom," Amber complained, "I was just going to—"

"Thank you, honey." She hooked her arm through her daughter's, then said to Noel, "I won't keep her long."

"Yes, ma'am," he said and watched the two ladies leave with a lot of regret.

Of course the second they were gone, the guys moved in.

Her brother, Garrett, a much larger, male version of Amber with the same dark hair and blue eyes, also happened to be his lieutenant at the fire station. Adam and Shohn were her cousins, and Gray was a cousin's husband. At least her father chose to join the elders near the grill. He could be thankful to be spared the scrutiny of her uncles Sawyer, Gabe and Jordan, and her much older cousin Casey.

When the others were close enough, Noel stuck out his hand, saying to Garrett, "Congratulations." The sooner he got this over with, the happier he'd be.

Garrett smiled with evil delight as he accepted the gesture, saying to his cousins, "Notice how he managed to spit that out without flinching?"

"Manned right up," Adam said.

Shohn slowly nodded. "He's still a little pale, though, don't you think?"

"I'm short on sleep," Noel said for the umpteenth time, even though he despised whining.

"So you like kids?" Garrett asked, then continued before he could answer, saying, "Good to know. Maybe I'll name you as a godparent—"

When Noel started choking again, the men all laughed.

Shohn sized him up critically. "Maybe you should break him in with some babysitting first."

"Me?" Noel asked, appalled at the idea. "What about you? You guys love kids!"

That took care of their smiles, turning them all solemn in a heartbeat.

Silence stretched out until Adam asked, his tone far too serious, "And you don't?"

He didn't like being cornered and wouldn't tolerate it. "I don't know kids. Never been around them."

"What about siblings?" Shohn asked.

"No."

"Aw, so he was an only child," Garrett said, mocking him in a way he found far more comfortable than the solemn scrutiny. "Must give you the willies being around a family as large as ours."

It did, not that he'd admit it. "I think of it as a party." True enough. A weekly freaking party. "And I don't get *the willies*."

"A party," Shohn repeated. "Like a holiday…or maybe a wedding?"

"No, wait," Adam said. "Parties end, right? Weddings do not. So—"

"No, they don't." They were having a fine time poking fun at him, but he'd had enough. "Did you guys want something?"

"Just to make sure you're okay," Adam said.

"You really did go pale," Shohn added. "Like someone had given you a…scare?"

"Didn't know you just needed a nap," Garrett added. "There's a lounge chair over there where the women are sitting if you want to rest up a bit."

Noel opened his mouth—and a badminton birdie hit Garrett in the shoulder, making him jump.

They all turned to see Tucker Turley, the sheriff, scowling at their cousin Kady, who tried to look innocent even while smothering her laugh.

Tucker said to the guys, "She has a good arm. At least, I don't think she was aiming for his head."

Kady waved her racket. "Stop picking on Noel before I tell Amber, and come play instead."

Garrett, wearing a huge grin now that he had a new focus, had already picked up the birdie and was striding their way. Shohn followed along, promising payback. Adam called out, "Kady's on my team," and he took off, too.

That left only Gray and he seemed in no hurry to leave.

Noel glanced at him in warning. Gray wasn't related to Amber except by marriage. Maybe that gave him a different outlook on things.

"It gets easier," Gray said.

"You think?" Because so far, from Noel's perspective, it had gotten more difficult. He liked them all. No problem there. But there were so many of them. He'd never known a family the size of hers, at least not where everyone was so close to everyone else, and in everyone's business, with love passed around without reserve.

They were pushy. And intrusive. And they seldom showed an ounce of discretion when butting in—

"They're overwhelming, I know. But they mean well." When Lisa came out of the house carrying a tray, surrounded by three dogs, Gray watched her with a small smile. "They push their way in and refuse to back off. But they're not judgmental, just protective. And they look out for each other. Amber especially brings it on herself with the way she interfered in all their lives." He glanced at Noel. "In *my* life."

"She enjoys meddling." But in Amber's case, it was always well-meaning, and she did have that crazy intuition to guide her, ensuring things turned out well. She'd been instrumental in matching up a lot of couples, Gray and Lisa included.

"That she does," Gray agreed. "And she's good at it." He hesitated. "Except when it comes to you."

"Me?" Noel scowled. Since Amber was the only woman he wanted, she didn't need to manipulate him. He'd made that clear to her, but he wouldn't explain himself to Gray.

"How long have you two been dating now?"

That sounded like a trick question and Noel ran a hand over his face. "Awhile," he said noncommittally. *Dating* was such a bland word. At first he and Amber had sparred, each trying to get the upper hand. Then they'd tentatively gotten together—and Noel knew his life would never be the same. They'd fallen into a comfortable, no-demands affair that really worked.

At least it worked for him. Was Amber dissatisfied? Did she want more from him?

If so, she could tell him herself, without the help of her entire family.

"I won't heckle you the way her brother and cousins do." Gray pushed away from the tree where he'd been leaning. "Instead I'll tell it to you straight. Amber is the heart of the family. They all adore her and want to shelter her. If she matters to you, you should think about what Amber wants and plan accordingly."

Provoked, Noel stiffened. "What the hell is that supposed to—"

But Gray walked away, his gaze snagged on his wife.

To hell with it. Noel dug the keys out of his pocket and started to leave, but at the last minute he went into the house to find Amber first.

She was alone in the kitchen, humming as she arranged condiments on a tray.

Noel soaked up the back view of her, her trim figure in sexy short-shorts that hugged her ass perfectly and a tank top that showcased her tiny waist. He even admired her dark hair in the loose braid and the set of her straight, proud shoulders.

Unable to resist, he stepped up close and slipped his hands around to her stomach. Nuzzling the side of her neck, he said, "I'm taking off."

Her head fell back to his shoulder. Seconds ticked by while he kissed the sensitive spot behind her ear. Then she whispered, "You're tired?"

Exhausted, but he said, "I'm fine."

"Then don't go." She turned in his arms and his hands just naturally fell to her hips.

She hooked her fingers in the front waistband of his shorts and tugged him closer in reprimand. "Don't let them run you off, okay?"

He could lose himself in those big blue eyes of hers. "It's a family thing," he said, meaning the celebration of a baby, "and I'm not family."

Amber slipped her hands inside his T-shirt, drawing them up and over his abs, which tightened in reaction.

Her touch never failed to fire his blood. He closed his eyes briefly, struggling to get a grip. Out of desperate need, he put his hands over hers and tried not to think about what he'd rather be doing. "You're killing me, Amber."

"Stay," she urged, "and in two hours we can leave together."

With a promise like that, how could he resist? He kissed her, then said against her lips, "Okay."

THE MOOD REMAINED festive as everyone celebrated the upcoming addition to the family.

Everyone but Noel.

Did he dislike kids? Or was it the commitment that came first that had him off-kilter today?

Amber watched him taking part in a game of badminton with several of the guys and a few of the women. He'd removed his shirt and it made her heart pound. When he grinned, she felt it clear to her toes.

"You should tell him how you feel."

She turned her head to see her dad standing close behind her. As she'd done all her life, she leaned on him and enjoyed the way his strong arms came around her.

Morgan propped his chin on her head and said, "Well?"

"He's never said how *he* feels."

"What law says a guy has to go first?"

"My law." Amber straightened, aware of Noel now watching her. He nearly got trampled because of his distraction, when Adam dived past him to return a volley. "Isn't he beautiful?"

Morgan laughed. "I can tell you think so."

She looked up at him. "What do you think, Dad? About him overall, I mean."

Without hesitation, Morgan said, "He's conscientious. That barn fire was dangerous, but Noel didn't hesitate, and because he knows what he's doing, he managed to not only save Fred, but his two cows and some chickens, too. If it hadn't been for Noel, Fred might have died." Under his breath, Morgan grumbled, "Damn fool had no business trying to burn the branches from that tree we trimmed. He's eighty now, you know. It's thanks to Noel that no one died."

Noel could have died, but Amber tried not to think about that. She worried enough for her brother. Luckily they'd managed the fire with no serious injuries. "He cares about animals."

"I'm sure Jordan knows and appreciates that."

Her uncle Jordan was a vet with a magical voice that could soothe the most fractious animals…and some humans, too.

"He's polite," Morgan continued. "Respectful of others. He takes care of himself and pitches in whenever anyone around town needs him."

So her dad saw all of Noel's sterling qualities, too? She sighed. "He's perfect."

Morgan sat at the side of a picnic table and drew her down beside him. "*Perfect* men don't faint over the mention of a baby."

"He didn't!" But it was close. "And you know what he thought, Dad. Any guy would have—"

"No," he corrected gently. "Not every guy would."

Amber had to give him that one. More than most men, her dad would understand surprise pregnancies.

"You're special," she said, leaning against his boulder shoulder. "You know that, right?"

"Loving you doesn't make me so. Not when it's so easy to do."

"Aww." She hugged his arm and thought how lucky she was that her mother had met her dad so long ago. "Thanks, Dad."

"Talk to him, honey. That's all I'm saying." Morgan tipped up her chin. "I see you going full-steam ahead, which is okay since I'm not sure you know any other way."

"It's part of my charm."

He chuckled. "Of course it is. But it'd be a good idea to find out if you're on the same tracks, right?"

Before she crashed. Amber frowned as she accepted the truth. "Okay. I'll talk to him tonight." Not that she was in any hurry to have kids. But yes, one day she wanted them.

That decision scared her silly. In all her twenty-seven years, she'd never fallen in love. Not until she met Noel Poet. Then she'd fallen hard and fast and now she couldn't imagine a life without him.

"Maybe you should do him a solid and get him out of here," Morgan said, "before Kady takes out his eye with that vicious swing of hers."

She saw that Noel was once again watching her instead of paying attention to the game. "All right. Soon as they finish up."

Just then he snapped back to attention, dived to the side and managed to return the birdie, which Shohn then missed.

After they all stopped cheering, she beckoned him over, and minutes later they were on the road.

CHAPTER TWO

IT WOULD HAVE been nice, Amber thought, to ride into town with Noel. If she had her way, they'd be spending a lot more time together.

Unfortunately, he could get called out if the station needed him, and she couldn't stay late, not when she had to open the bookstore early tomorrow morning. So far their romance, what there was of it, had been pieced together in the name of convenience.

Convenience had certainly worked for her. But what if that was all it was?

No, Noel cared more than that, she was sure of it. Tonight, she'd nail him down and get some answers. She had the drive to think about what exactly to say, but also to anticipate every possible response he might make, from the unthinkable to the expected.

Her dad and Uncle Sawyer lived further from town with joined property on the lake. Uncle Jordan and Georgia lived out a ways too, but not on the lake. Uncle Gabe and Elizabeth were in town, and Casey and Emma lived on the opposite side of the lake. Just about anywhere she went in Buckhorn, she was likely to run into eagle-eyed family.

Given the circumstances, an intrusion might have been welcome, a way to delay the inevitable. Of course this was one of the few times she *didn't* see anyone familiar and by the time they'd reached the small house Noel had recently purchased, she'd worked herself into a frenzy.

She was a woman who faced issues head-on, and she wanted this particular issue resolved…to her satisfaction.

Now that she'd made up her mind to force Noel to confront, and admit to, his feelings, only the tiniest doubt worried through her brain.

Tiny doubts, she realized, were not her forte.

He parked before her, then got out and came around to open her door.

Neighbors waved to them, a dog barked in the fenced yard next door and kids ran past in a game of tag.

Watching her closely, those velvety brown eyes of his alert, Amber wondered if he sensed her determination.

Likely. From the beginning, Noel had always been highly attuned to her.

He took her hand in his, reminding her of his size, how much larger and stronger he was—and how much it thrilled her. Going through the garage entrance, he led her into the kitchen.

She'd helped him choose this house, and in her mind she'd seen it as a starter home for a family.

Their family.

Three small bedrooms, a respectably sized kitchen and breakfast nook, and the open great room, large enough for a group of ten or more to gather together.

She'd pictured dinners with her family visiting, maybe another dog or two…and kids.

Turning her at the island that separated the kitchen from the great room, Noel caught her hips and put his forehead to hers.

She waited for his kiss, but instead he said, "I still smell like smoke. Want to join me in another shower?"

Yes. But she hesitated. Once they got in the shower, she'd give up her promise to her dad and nothing would get settled. So instead she pushed him back a few inches and said, "Let's talk first and shower after."

His gaze narrowed, then he stepped back, putting some space between them.

It wasn't only physical, Amber knew. She felt the emotional chasm as well and she didn't like it. "Don't look so glum, Noel. I'm not going to propose."

His eyes narrowed more. "I'm not glum."

"Baloney. You're braced like you think I plan to attack."

He shrugged. "I know your moods, Amber. You're definitely in attack mode. Given the day we've had and how your family came after me, I expect to be jumped any minute now."

Not liking that distance between them, she again caught the front waistband of his shorts and drew him back to her. She loved being held against his hard body, the heat of him, the smell of his skin. "I thought you liked it when I jumped you."

"Yeah," he said, his voice going husky with suggestion. "How about you get naked first, though?"

She laughed with the pleasure of being wanted by Noel. "For what I have in mind, it's better if we keep on our clothes."

Just that quickly, he retreated again, his gaze now challenging. He said nothing.

So the ball was in her court, huh? Fine. She wasn't a wimp. She could handle it.

Cuddling against him, she murmured, "If I talk about the future, will you go all stiff again?"

His hand slid down to her bottom and he said, "I'm already *stiff*, and it doesn't have a damn thing to do with talking."

"Mmm. So you are." He knew exactly how to sidetrack her…but not this time. She tilted up her face to see him. His dark eyes, such a sexy contrast from his fair hair, stared down into hers, waiting with a level of patience that often frustrated her. "You are such a beautiful man."

His mouth curled in an amused smile. "Beautiful, huh? With my hairy legs and five-o'clock shadow?"

Amber nodded. "And your dark eyes and buff body and—" she touched a fingertip to his mouth and sighed "—your crooked smile."

He lightly bit her fingertip. "Dare I hope that this is what you wanted to talk about?"

Blast. He'd sidetracked her after all. With a wince, she said, "Not exactly."

"No, I didn't think so." Stepping away from her again, he pulled out a stool at the island, offered it to her, then took one of his own.

She saw the exhaustion in his face and wondered how much sleep he'd gotten. As he'd said, showering after the fire hadn't completely rid him of the scent. Every so often she detected the faint odor of smoke still clinging to his body.

Knowing she couldn't keep him waiting, she said, "It's not about marriage."

Humor lit his eyes. "Yet somehow the word keeps popping up."

That made her scowl. Despite his obvious amusement, she'd heard the cynicism in his tone and darn it, she resented it. She propped her hands on her hips. "I guess you're one of those guys who is determined to stay single?"

That grin she loved graced his face. In the next second he'd hauled her in between his spread knees and had his mouth on hers. Warm, firm lips moved over hers until she opened. He licked in, his tongue teasing hers, stroking, melting her bones.

What did that kiss mean?

When he rocked her against his erection, she had her answer.

He eased up enough to say, "I know you like to do things your own way, honey. But how about you give me a chance to offer before you start insisting?"

Meaning he would be offering? Obviously she'd lied, to herself and him, when she'd said this wasn't about marriage, and now her heart soared, more so when his kiss turned consuming.

She started to lean back, to question him, to maybe cheer, but with his hands on her, one open on the back of her neck, the other over her backside, she couldn't budge.

He lifted her as he stood, her body held flush against his, and started down the hall to his bedroom without breaking that deep kiss. Amber wrapped her legs around his waist, and oh wow, the friction was *amazing.*

He'd obviously forgotten his shower and she didn't care. Noel always smelled good.

There was more she needed to talk about, but she'd have plenty of time later to get to it. Much later.

They went down on the bed together, Noel over her,

her legs still around him. God, how she loved the press of his weight.

He freed her mouth to trail hot kisses down her neck, then curled her toes with a growling love bite against the sensitive spot where her shoulder started.

Rising to his elbows, which pressed his lower body more firmly against the open juncture of her legs, he asked gruffly, "We're good now?"

With his dark gaze holding her captive, her whole body tingling at the feel of his erection, his words didn't register.

Amber tried to bring his mouth back to hers.

Resisting, he said, "Your talk?" He kissed the bridge of her nose, her chin, her mouth again. "You said it wasn't about marriage, but—"

Dazed, needy, she touched her fingertips to his bristly jaw. "It was about kids."

He went utterly still.

Lost to lust, Amber barely noticed. She trailed her touch to his thick hair, then around to his neck. "Noel…" she whispered, wanting him now.

"You're not pregnant."

"No." Not yet, she wasn't. She leaned up and nipped his bottom lip. "I'm not talking about kids right now. But someday—"

"I don't want any."

Hearing the implacability in that stark statement, Amber dropped back to the pillow.

Staring up at him, she tried to decipher the joke—not that he'd sounded joking. But…he had to be.

"Ever?" she teased, waiting for his smile, his reassurance.

Without blinking, he confirmed, "Ever."

The lust withered. He couldn't mean that. Okay, so he wasn't ready to settle down right now. She could handle that. But to *never* want children of his own?

Emotions flitted over his face, wariness, regret and then resolve. He bent to her neck again at the same time his hand curved over her breast. "I care about you, Amber. You know that."

He *cared*? What did that even mean? She wanted his love, a future together.

A family.

She felt his hot breath on her ear, then the touch of his tongue, and she shivered. He couldn't expect her to do this now. "*Wait—*"

His mouth covered hers, and holy smoke, he put his all into that kiss, drugging her with flaring need.

She realized her legs were still around his waist. He must have, too, given the way he slowly rocked against her. Added to the hand now caressing her breast, the thumb stroking over her nipple, and she lost her resistance in under five seconds.

Her body gave up before her mind, but her mind hadn't lagged far behind.

When Noel levered up enough to tug off his shirt, she helped him, wanting to feel the heat of his skin, the bulk of his muscles and that crisp chest hair. Soon as he came back down to her, she stroked her hands over his shoulders to his back, down his spine to his taut behind.

He groaned…

And her cell phone buzzed in her pocket.

Pressed so close together, they both felt it.

His second groan was out of frustration. "Ignore it," he whispered. "It's probably just your family."

"Just let me check," she whispered, squirming

enough to retrieve the phone from her pocket. Her family knew she'd be with Noel and wouldn't call without reason. She looked at the caller ID and smiled. It was the next best thing to family. "Give me one second, okay? I promise to make it quick."

He pressed his mouth to hers, lingering for a heartbeat, then sat up and away. "On some things," he said, "I'm more than willing to compromise."

His comment abruptly reminded her of his absurd claims. Never have children? Ridiculous. Somehow she'd figure it out.

Mocked by a twist of fate, she accepted the call from her best friend, Peggy Gold…mother of a fifteen-month-old daughter. Amber adored the little girl, everything about her.

But Noel never wanted children.

Without looking at him, she mustered up a happy tone and said into her cell, "How's my favorite little girl?"

She pictured baby June with the adorable dimples in her chubby cheeks, how she would squeal, racing forward in her haphazard way, grasping at the air in her rush to reach Amber.

But it wasn't Peggy who answered. "Amber? Amber Hudson?"

Alarm went up her spine and she slowly slid to the side of the bed to stand. "Yes?" She was aware of Noel, also, becoming alert.

"I'm sorry, Ms. Hudson, but I have some very distressing news to share with you."

NOEL WATCHED HER face go blank, saw her blindly reach for something solid. He caught her hand and guided her back to sit on the side of the bed. Scooting around beside her, he stayed close, wanting to finish what they'd started, out of lust, yes, but also from a driving need to seal the deal, to confirm that things wouldn't change between them.

For now, the call took priority. He couldn't hear the other side of the conversation, but Amber's questions and responses told him someone had been hurt.

His chest tightened in dread. "Your family?"

She shook her head, then clutched his hand in hers. He went one further and put his other arm around her, surrounding her as much as he could, doing his best to lend her his strength.

"I'll be there as soon as I can. Yes, today," she promised. "I'll leave as quickly as I can, but it'll still take me a couple of hours… Yes, okay. Thank you."

Leave? To go where?

Heart thumping heavily, Noel waited until she'd disconnected the call, but the second she did she was on the go, shoving the phone back into her pocket and hurrying out of his bedroom.

Urgency filled her expression, making her all but blind to him.

He caught her at the door leading out to the garage. "Whoa. Slow down, honey. Tell me what's wrong."

As if she'd only then remembered him, she stared at him blankly. "I have to go."

"Okay," he said calmly. "Tell me where."

"My friend…" She gulped deep breaths.

When he started to hug her, she pushed away. "Don't!" She stared at him, appalled, then explained, "If you do that, I'll get weepy, and I can't be weepy right now."

Holding up his hands, his tone as gentle as he could make it, Noel said, "All right, no touching. But take a moment and tell me what's happened."

"My friend Peggy."

"Peggy Gold, right? Nice smile, short brown hair."

"And green eyes."

He didn't remember her eyes, but then, any woman who stood next to Amber tended to disappear—at least for him. "Yeah, I met her a few times. I think it was at the bookstore once, and then at your house a few times."

Amber nodded. "She has a daughter."

"I remember." Cute little girl, but Noel had deliberately steered clear of the child. Then a thought struck him. God, he hoped she wasn't hurt.

"She's in the hospital and it's bad."

It felt like his heart hit his feet and all the oxygen left his brain. "The baby...?"

"No." She took in his reaction with awed speculation, then shook her head. "Peggy. A car accident... June wasn't with her..." She gave up on explanations. "I have to go."

Again Noel caught her arm. "June is the baby?"

"Yes. She was with the sitter. Peggy was on her way home from work." Her lip trembled before she flattened her mouth. *"I have to go."*

Noel held on to her. "You're shaking." Knowing that the baby was okay helped him to regain his composure. "Let me drive you."

She gave him an unreadable look, shook her head and said, "She moved a month ago and now lives almost an hour from here. I don't know how long I'm going to stay, and you'll have to work."

No, he thought, his mind rebelling. She couldn't go

like this. "I'll drive you and then come back." Along the way, he could at least explain…what? How did a man explain something that he couldn't bear to talk about?

Amber refused him. "You're sweet, but I don't have time for this. Please, Noel, just let me go."

Let her go? Why did she say that with so much inevitability? He sought the right words to convince her, but Amber didn't give him a chance to speak.

"You know me. I'll be fine. I always am." She backed up to the door, opened it. At the last second, she said, "I love you." Then she was gone.

Noel stood there, rooted to the spot. She'd made that pronouncement so casually, as if it weren't life-altering, as if it didn't take his breath away.

Amber loved him… He'd waited a long time to hear that, but now that he had, desperation gripped him.

Would her love for him be enough to keep her?

WHILE DRIVING HOME to pack a bag, Amber stayed busy making arrangements. Her cousin Shohn's wife, Nadine, agreed to take care of her boxer. Rookie loved visiting Nadine's pet hotel, Animal House. Some of his best friends were there, and while she knew he'd miss her, he'd also have a great time.

Next she called her cousin Adam. As an elementary-school gym teacher, he had some time off in the summer and could go to the bookstore to rearrange her schedule to accommodate a few days off. He also knew her two part-time employees and would be able to get in touch with them for her.

Lastly she called her mom and dad and explained what had happened. Like Noel, Morgan tried to convince her that he should do the driving for her. After trying to deny him, unsuccessfully since she wasn't quite up to her usual brass, it was Misty who insisted that he let her be.

Her mother understood that while she wasn't a crier, too much coddling during an emotionally difficult time could absolutely shake her foundation.

Rookie, thrilled to see her when she got home, used his doggy door to shoot in from the backyard, slid across the kitchen floor and plowed into her with enthusiasm.

Amber sank to her knees. "Hey, bud. I missed you, too." He licked her face while crawling into her lap, his whole body jiggling. This was the routine they went through every workday, though usually on a weekend gathering at her dad's or her uncle Sawyer's house, she'd have taken Rookie along. She'd only left him behind this time because she'd hoped to spend a few hours with Noel, and she'd assumed she and the dog would have the evening together.

Rookie followed her around the house while she hastily packed a few things for an overnight stay. She was just about to go when her brother showed up. Garrett knocked, then came in without waiting for her to answer. He didn't give her a chance to dodge him, either, drawing her into his arms and giving her a tight hug, then quickly setting her back before she could well up over it.

More than anyone else, her brother knew her well.

"Dad told me what happened. I came to pick up Rookie for you so you could get on the road."

"You'll take him to Nadine?"

"The park first, then to Nadine."

That was almost more consideration than she could

take. She started to thank him, but her throat felt too tight, so she only nodded and handed him Rookie's leash.

After fastening it on the dog, he asked, "You have enough cash on you? A full tank of gas? Your credit card?"

Again she nodded and finally found her voice. "Yes. I'm all set." Then with a little of her old sass, she added, "I'm not incompetent."

"Far from it, sis, but you're understandably upset, so if you need anything else, just let me know." With his free hand, he picked up her suitcase and carried it out, Rookie following along from the end of the leash.

Just as they got to her truck, Adam pulled up and he had Shohn with him.

Amber rolled her eyes. With a choked laugh, she complained, "You guys."

They knew to avoid emotional excesses and instead greeted Rookie to give her a little time.

When he straightened, Shohn asked, "Got your phone charger?"

"I keep an extra in my car."

Garrett nodded. "Don't worry about anything here, okay? We've got it covered."

"Thanks. I'll check in when I can."

"That'd be nice," he said, smoothing down her braid. "Mom and Dad like to worry."

Garrett liked to worry, too, but she didn't say so. "I have to go."

Giving her a brief hug, he said near her ear, "I hope everything turns out okay."

She nodded, squeezed him back, then stepped away

to give Rookie a hug. It was nice that her dog loved all the family as much as she did.

Adam opened her truck door and she got in, then paused. Not looking at any of them, she said, "I love you guys."

"Drive safe."

"Drive *slow*."

"Don't get distracted."

They were crazy and, yes, intrusive.

As Amber pulled away, she wondered what she'd do without them.

BY THE HOUR, Noel's frustration mounted.

He didn't know what to think. Three days had gone by and he still hadn't spoken with Amber. He'd called her and gotten her voice mail. She'd returned his call and, since he was working, she'd left a message. A bland, impersonal message that could have been from a neighbor.

Sorry I missed you. Things are...not good here. I won't burden you with details, just know that I'm okay but it might be a few more days before I get home. Gotta go now. Bye.

That was it. Nothing else. *I won't burden you?* What the hell was that supposed to mean? They were a couple. She couldn't burden him, not by sharing her worries.

Not by sharing herself.

When he'd called her back, it had gone straight to voice mail again.

She'd claimed to love him!

Once. Only that once—on her way out the door.

But that was three days ago and since then they'd

played phone tag to the point he was ready to go after her.

When Garrett returned to the station after a community meeting, Noel zeroed in on him. He'd bet her brother had talked to her. In fact, he was sure of it.

If nothing else, Garrett could tell him where to find her, so Noel gave up on his light-housekeeping duty—a chore they all shared and one he'd get back to after he gained some answers—and headed for Garrett's office.

The door was open, so he didn't bother knocking, just said, "Got a minute?"

Garrett glanced up. He stood behind his desk, returning files to a drawer. "I've got five, then I'm working out before inspections. What's up?"

Noel propped a shoulder against the doorframe. All firefighters maintained a level of physical fitness through workouts, so unless a call came in, they all allotted time for training and daily housekeeping.

If he'd known Garrett was headed there next, he could have gone along and casually brought up Amber... No, screw that. He didn't feel casual, and he wouldn't dance around it. "Where is your sister?"

Garrett stopped fiddling with the files and, brows raised, gave Noel his undivided attention. "You don't know?"

Did he have to sound so disbelieving? "I know she got a call about her friend Peggy and that she was going to her. But we keep missing each other's calls."

Closing the desk drawer and folding his arms over his chest, Garrett said, "And she didn't leave you a message?"

"She did."

"And?"

And she hadn't told him anything. "Look, I'm worried about her."

"Me, too." Garrett started out of the room, saying as he went, "Amber should be home tomorrow."

Well, that was good news. "What time?"

"Later in the day. I'm sure she'll catch you up then—" he stopped in front of Noel "—and tell you anything she wants you to know."

Noel straightened. "What the hell does that mean?"

"It means if my sister wanted to talk to you, she would."

"I told you. We keep missing—"

"She knows your schedule, Noel, same as she knows mine. She hasn't had any trouble getting in touch with me."

True, and it burned his ass big-time. "You're saying there are things happening with Amber, but you won't tell me?"

Garrett shrugged. "Not my place." But he unbent enough to ask, "What'd you do to get cut out?"

At least a dozen times a day, Noel had chewed over the last conversation they'd had. He'd told her that he never wanted kids, but not why. And worse, he'd taken away her opportunity to talk to him about it. Guilt added to his irritation, so he growled, "None of your damn business."

Garrett laughed. "You came to me, remember." And he started out of the room.

Noel said, "Just tell me if she's okay?"

"You know my sister. She's a rock. No matter what happens, she's always okay."

"You said you were worried."

Garrett gave him a dead stare. "Yeah, but I love her, so I'm allowed."

As Noel watched Garrett leave, he assured himself that things couldn't be too bad, or her brother would look more upset.

I love her, so I'm allowed.

Damn it, he loved her, too. He hadn't yet had a chance to tell her, though. In the larger scheme of things, would it matter?

Tomorrow couldn't get here soon enough to suit him.

Tomorrow, they'd talk and somehow he'd work it all out.

CHAPTER THREE

AMBER HADN'T HAD much time to think, not with everything happening at Mach speed, but in times like these, thinking could be overrated. There was too much to do, too much to *feel*, too many overwhelming emotions, some of them tragic, some poignant. She was immeasurably sad, insanely busy, but also feeling blessed.

Most of all, she was honored.

It had taken some fast talking to convince her parents and Garrett that she didn't need or want a visit on her first night back. Often, after being out of town, she'd stay the night with her parents and let them dote on her. Her dad, especially, enjoyed making and sharing pancakes in the morning. And she and her mom would sit on the front porch and chat quietly over coffee.

This time, she honestly didn't think she had the energy for it.

Tomorrow would be soon enough to go over everything, and she expected her whole big, wonderful family to show up in force, insisting on helping in a dozen different ways.

Because they abided by her wishes, usually anyway, it surprised Amber to realize a truck was parked at the curb in front of her house. When she got closer and recognized the truck, conflicting emotions swamped her.

He was here.

And now she'd have to deal with him sooner rather than later.

At the very least, she needed a good night's sleep before choking down his "no kids" rule. Yet the second her headlights showed, he stepped out of his truck and stared toward her, watching her approach.

Well, no time like the present, then, she decided. Not that she had a choice anyway. She couldn't exactly race him into the house and lock the door behind her. Not when it was going to take her easily three trips to unload the bed of her truck.

Her thoughts scrambled from happy to see him, to dread over their confrontation, before settling into annoyance. She parked in the driveway, glanced into the rear seat of her crew-cab truck and quietly exited.

Noel was already at her truck door and before she could say "Hello," or "Get lost," or ask a single question, he had her locked against him in his strong, unbreakable hold.

God, it felt good to have his arms around her, like truly coming home.

Without any other greeting, he took her mouth, gently coaxing her lips to part so his tongue could play with hers.

It never failed.

Every clear thought, every bit of situational awareness, evaporated. Amber knew she leaned into him, knew she snaked her arms around his neck.

Knew she kissed him back.

"I missed you," he whispered, then immediately kissed her again.

The sudden loud screech from the second seat had him jumping back. It was almost comical, the horrified look on his face as understanding and denial stirred together.

Amber put a finger to the center of his chest, said "Excuse me" and stepped him back out of her way.

The second she had the door open and saw that small, precious face scrunched up, her heart turned over. "It's okay, June Bug. I didn't forget about you, I promise." She opened the restraints on the car seat and, girding herself for Noel's reaction, lifted out her bundle.

He still appeared staggered. "That's a baby!"

"Is it?" Amber said, looking down as if in surprise. "Junie, honey, are you a baby?"

June stared at Noel in the light from the open truck door. Silky brown hair curled around her face, her eyes, a soft shade of blue, unblinking. Because she didn't know Noel and she'd had so many changes lately, she dropped her head to Amber's shoulder, half hiding while keeping her gaze on Noel. In a whisper, she squeaked, "Bebe."

"That's right," Amber said. "You are a baby, aren't you?" She brushed a kiss over the sweet-smelling hair and gave Noel a pointed look. "You should probably go. It's okay, you know. I've got this."

He hadn't looked away from June yet.

June hadn't looked away from him, either.

"Noel," she repeated, doing her best to stay strong. "You need to go. As you can see, I've got a lot to do."

That shook him free and he glanced at her, but only for a second, before returning his attention to June. "What's going on here?"

She couldn't explain, not in front of June. The baby wouldn't understand much, but Amber wasn't willing to take the chance. "You know why I left."

"To help your friend—"

She interrupted with a shake of her head, doing her best to tamp down the tears that came each and every time she thought of Peggy. "There wasn't anything to be done by the time I got there."

Noel stared at her a moment, then cupped his hand to her cheek. "God, honey, I'm so sorry."

Stepping away, she said, "Remember what sympathy does to me. Can't have that right now." She kissed June again, who still stared at Noel with her fixed gaze. "You might as well know, I'm keeping her."

His eyes flared.

So that he didn't misunderstand, she said, "June Bug is mine now."

And the baby, still in her sweet, unsure voice, repeated "Mine," as if to make sure he got it.

NOEL FINISHED SETTING up the crib in Amber's bedroom. Her house was smaller than his with only two bedrooms, and the second bedroom was in use as a walk-in closet. She hadn't wanted him to help, she'd made that much clear. If she'd gotten her way—something she was used to with everyone else—she'd have sent him packing there in the driveway after dropping her little bombshell.

How she'd have handled it all herself, he didn't know. But she would have, that much he knew with certainty. Amber was the most resourceful woman he'd ever known.

But just because she could, didn't mean she should.

So he'd insisted on unloading her truck first. Car seat, high chair, stroller, crib…and those were just the bulkiest items. Boxes and boxes of diapers, tubs of clothes, more tubs of toys. He didn't know where to put it all, and Amber was on the couch, rocking a sleepy June, so he didn't ask her for direction.

With each trip he'd taken out to her truck, he'd seen her there, the baby curled in her arms as she gently rocked, rocked, rocked…as if she'd been born to it, like fate had intended her to be in that exact spot, doing that exact thing.

But fate sure as hell hadn't intended him to be an observer.

And until she'd fallen asleep, June's gaze had tracked him without blinking each time he'd passed through, then returned.

Getting the crib assembled wasn't the problem, but doing so silently had challenged him. He'd managed because he didn't want to wake the baby.

When she locked on to him with those big blue eyes, he felt it clear down to his soul. It unnerved him, damn it. Better to let her sleep and spare him the discomfort.

With the bed together, he found a crib sheet in one of the tubs of folded clothes and put it on, then found a light cotton blanket, too.

Out of necessity, given the small size of the room, the crib sat very close to Amber's bed. Noel thought of Amber curled up there, and it should have been an enticing image…but not with a baby's bed three feet away. He turned to leave the room—only to find Amber standing there, a limp-limbed June Bug in her arms.

"She only weighs thirty pounds," Amber whispered, "but she's getting heavy." With a tight smile, she added, "So move."

With alacrity, Noel edged out of the way, yet he couldn't make himself leave. He stood behind Amber, watching as she eased her sleepy burden into the crib, then just as silently pulled up the side rail. She put the soft blanket over June's dimpled legs, kissed her smooshed-up cheek and, looking wearier than he'd ever seen her, walked past him out of the room.

Noel couldn't seem to get his feet to budge. Couldn't budge his gaze, either. It stayed on the baby, on the way her little rosebud mouth puckered a few times, how her little chubby fist opened and closed before going lax again.

Objectively, he knew she was a beautiful little girl. Emotionally, it didn't matter what she looked like.

She was a baby and she scared him half to death.

He found Amber in the kitchen emptying a box of bibs, blunt-tipped forks and suction-bottomed bowls, along with what he assumed to be June's favorite foods.

"You should get some sleep. You look beat."

"True," she said without looking at him. "But even if she sleeps the rest of the night, which is doubtful, she'll be up bright and early and I'd rather be a little organized."

Noel walked over beside her and rested a hip against the counter, his arms folded over his chest. "What did you mean, she's yours?"

"Exactly that." She finished emptying one box, broke it down and put it in a stack, then started on another.

"For how long?"

Those brilliant sapphire eyes, now a little bloodshot, slanted his way. "Mine is mine, Noel. Forever."

He couldn't believe that, but clearly she was in an obstinate mood. He wasn't sure how to proceed, but he definitely didn't want to exacerbate things. Calmly, gently, he asked, "Will you tell me about it?"

"I won't go into to nitty-gritty detail. No offense, but I don't have time. The overview, though, is that Peggy... didn't survive." Her voice faded to a whisper. "I didn't make it in time to see her."

More than ever he wished he'd gone along with her. "I'm sorry."

She acknowledged that with a nod. "She had a will and named me guardian. June's father wanted no part of her and gave up his rights long ago. Her parents are there, but her mother had a stroke a few months back, her father has his hands full, and they know I would never try to cut them out, so they didn't protest."

Noel's heart ached for her, though she was powering through without an excess of emotion.

Hefting another box onto the counter, she tore into it, rearranging her own cabinets as she did so to fit in everything. "Peggy didn't have much, but once I can get better organized, I'll get the rest of June's things, including her dresser and some larger toys, and Peggy's minivan. I took everything I figured was essential in this trip."

Things couldn't possibly have changed so much, so quickly. Noel's head was swimming, so how must she feel?

Amber finished that box, too, and headed into the living room.

Noel followed. When she started to lift the high chair, he caught her arm and turned her to face him. "Slow down, please."

She stared at his chest through two complete, deep breaths, then looked up at him and managed a strained smile. "You should go. You'll have to be at the station tomorrow—"

"No, I switched to have the day off." Because he'd wanted to be with her.

She patted his chest in regret. "I'm sorry. As you can see, I'm slammed." Her hand stayed on his chest, subtly caressing until she caught herself and drew it away. "Plus I have a baby now. I know how you feel about that."

He ignored the snide comment. "You can't do this by yourself."

"Of course I can. But you know my family, Noel. Do you really think I'll have to?"

No, she wouldn't. Her family shoved their way in through thick or thin, there to celebrate the good times and to help get through the difficulties. "I guess not."

"They'll all converge tomorrow." Before he could wonder about that, she explained, "I insisted I wanted some peace and quiet tonight."

"Fine." But he was here *now*, damn it. "Until then, let me help."

She glared up at the ceiling, appeared to count, then pointed down the hall. "There is a baby. In my room." She went on tiptoes to say directly into his face, "You don't like babies, remember?"

And again she tried to march away.

He drew her back around, and since it usually worked, he kissed her to get her attention.

This time was no different.

She didn't push him away, but she did try to poker up on him…only it didn't last, and when she softened against him, her body sighing into his, he forced himself to stop. "You can't get that close to me and expect me to resist."

Her tone and expression seductive, she whispered, "I was blasting you."

God, he loved her many moods, and he especially loved the way she reacted to him. From the beginning, he'd only found one way to sidetrack her and luckily it worked like a charm. "I felt your breath, knew your lips were right there, and it didn't matter what you were saying."

"Oh." The heaviness left her eyes and she became more alert.

He still held her upper arms so she couldn't storm away from him again. "Listen up, okay? I don't dislike babies."

"I did not dream that, Noel. You said a very clear *never* to the idea of children."

"True, I don't want kids." That hadn't changed. "But I want *you*."

"I," she stated, exasperation replacing the sensual haze, "now come with a kid."

He'd need more time to think about that. She would, too. Her friend had passed away, she'd taken on a massive responsibility, and she had to be reeling, regardless of how stoic she appeared right now. "We're in a relationship."

"Are we?" She put her forehead to his chest and let out a long breath. "I'm not holding you to anything, okay? You can go with a clear conscience."

Just like that? She expected him to walk out on her, to give up everything they had and leave her to deal alone?

Did she think he stuck around out of some misguided Good Samaritan sensibility? That assumption pissed him off. "Stop it, Amber."

"Look around you! I have so much to do. I need a shower. And I'm really hoping to grab a few hours of sleep."

He glided his fingers over her smooth cheek, down to her chin to tip up her face. "Sleep has been difficult, I imagine."

She didn't quite meet his gaze. "June's routine has been completely destroyed, and she's seldom slept more than a few hours at a time."

"So tell you what." He cupped her precious face in his hands and bent his knees to look into her eyes. "Let's compromise here a little, okay? You go take your shower while I put things away." Stubborn pride would only take her so far, and while she might call the shots with her family, he wasn't that easy. "I'm not leaving, so you may as well put me to work."

She rubbed her forehead. "Fine." In rapid order she told him where he should fit everything. The majority of June's clothes and toys would stay in the storage tubs for now, and those would go in her guest-bedroom-slash-closet. The high chair would go in the kitchen, of course, the stroller in the garage. The playpen anywhere in the living area where it would fit—as long as it was away from electrical cords, shelves and anything else she might be able to reach.

"I can handle that," he promised. "Go, relax, and if she wakes I'll come tell you."

Amber lifted her chin. "I'm locking the door, so just knock."

Stubborn. "You think this is all a ploy to get you naked? If it was, I could probably just kiss you and—"

"Behave!" She made a hasty retreat directly into the

bathroom, closing and locking the door behind her. Seconds later he heard the shower start.

Still grinning, Noel made short work of putting everything away. Amber remained in the shower.

He wondered if she'd eaten, decided she probably hadn't and made her a grilled cheese sandwich.

She was still in the shower.

He had the food on the table and was pacing when the bathroom door finally opened. Amber's dark hair was in a towel, another towel wrapped around her body.

Knowing she was naked under that towel, seeing her long, slim legs bare, sent an avalanche of need coursing through his blood.

"I forgot to get clothes," she explained, her voice sounding funny. "I'm afraid if I go in my room now, I might wake—"

She no sooner said it than they both heard June saying, "Baba, ba ba, babababa."

Amber didn't move. In fact she seemed to slump more.

"What's she saying?" Noel asked.

"She wants her bottle."

And that was a problem? Trying to be helpful, he said, "I know right where it is."

Amber lifted her face, and he got his first good look at her eyes.

She'd been crying.

His strong, indomitable, take-charge Amber... reduced to tears?

That was why she'd showered so long. He should have realized. The past five days had been hell for her. The rush to her friend's hospital bed, a funeral, guardianship.

If he tried to hold her, which he desperately wanted to do, she might turn away from him. Or completely lose control.

He wasn't sure which would be worse.

"What can I do?"

"You can go."

That little quaver in her voice nearly did him in. "I'm not leaving, so stop trying to shove me out the door." Sometimes with Amber the best defense was to take charge—so that she couldn't.

Taking her arm and leading her toward the bedroom, Noel said, "Find your pajamas. I'll get the bottle ready. Milk? Juice? What does she prefer?"

"Usually just water at bedtime, but tonight everything is so screwed up I planned to give her milk."

"I'll get it."

"But—"

"No buts."

It pleased him when she gave in, even though it also proved she was off-kilter in a big way. Otherwise it never would have happened.

At least he was staying, Noel thought. He'd count that as a win.

He got Amber into the bedroom, started to go…and June saw him. She locked eyes with him, smiled and lifted her arms in demand.

Best-laid plans…

KNOWING HOW NOEL felt, and knowing she couldn't take having him partially involved but not fully committed, Amber rushed around in front of him.

"You little stinker," she said to June and lifted her.

June pushed away from her unexpectedly, and in

her rush to hold on to the baby, Amber almost lost her towel. It took some fast maneuvering to set the baby back down and grab it in time.

She was pretty sure Noel got a flash of her backside. Not the first time, but it was the first in a situation like this.

She absolutely would not make eye contact with him.

June stepped back, her expression pugnacious, and reached for Noel again.

"She's fine," Amber said, securing the towel the best she could. Finally she glanced at Noel. "Just go on and I'll get dressed and then bring her in."

Looking appalled, especially with the way June stared at him, Noel nodded. "Okay, sure."

Amber watched his antics, how he began to back up, step by slow step.

When he had only one foot out the door, June bellowed. For such a tiny little girl, she really had a big voice.

Noel stopped dead in his tracks.

Appeased, June fell silent, but again held up her arms.

Huh, Amber thought. She took in Noel's stricken expression, trying to align it with his self-professed aversion to children. She lifted a brow. "I won't get dressed until you're out of here."

"I've seen you naked—"

"Shh!" Ridiculously, her face flamed. "Don't talk about *that* in front her."

He snorted, but said without total conviction, "She's a baby. She doesn't understand."

"Well, I do." Amber pointed for the door. "Just go."

The second he moved, June's bottom lip trembled and she wound herself up, preparing for a real explosion.

"She won't let me."

Amber rolled her eyes. "As you just pointed out, she's a baby. She can't stop you."

Yet the second he shifted away, June wailed again.

Half in, half out of the door, Noel scowled, waffled a moment in pained indecision, then strode forward with purpose.

June bounced in excitement and held up her arms. "Baba ba babba ba."

"Well," Amber said, watching the careful way he lifted the baby. "She knows what she wants."

And, she thought, maybe Noel *didn't* know what he wanted. Not really.

She watched Noel hold June out the length of his long arms, which made all those impressive muscles flex. It was an awkward hold, yet June didn't seem to mind. She pumped her legs and laughed.

What was it about a man and baby? The sight of them together led a hardwired charge straight to a woman's heart.

"What do I do with her?"

He already held the baby, and no way could she remove that image from her memory banks. It was something she'd see even in her sleep.

Darn it, after what he'd said, she'd wanted to keep a physical separation there. She didn't want to see him holding the baby. Witnessing it was bound to be a detriment to her emotional well-being.

Well, she could at least keep the contact brief. With that uppermost in mind, Amber steered him toward the door. "Give me three minutes to throw on clothes."

Stiff-armed, he nodded. "Okay." Keeping June straight out in front of him like a nautical figurehead on a human ship, he left the room.

Amber closed the door and collapsed back against it, but not for long. If she stopped moving, she started thinking, and that led to a loss of control.

It was bad enough that she'd lingered in the shower, giving in to the useless tears. With new purpose, she hurried to her dresser.

Haste got her back out of the room in under two minutes. Wearing flannel pants and a loose T-shirt, her hair still in a towel, she charged into the room... and found Noel sitting cross-legged on the floor in front of the playpen.

Playing peekaboo.

June stood inside, her diaper so soggy it hung to her knees, but she laughed at every face Noel made.

He'd all but filled the playpen with soft stuffed toys. June ignored them all as Noel peeked over the top rail, then under it, a game she obviously enjoyed.

That big faker.

Regardless of any contrary claims he'd made, Amber couldn't believe Noel disliked children. He was already too concerned and too engaged.

While June laughed, he said, "We're good if you want to dry your hair."

Un-freaking-believable. What did he mean, messing with her head like this? "Her diaper is soaked."

Cringing dramatically, he said, "Yeah, I noticed. But a diaper change is beyond me."

"Did you get her bottle?"

He shrugged one hard shoulder. "No. She seemed to forget about it."

"So let me do that first, then I'll change her." She hurried into the kitchen—and there on the table she found nirvana in the form of a golden grilled cheese sandwich, chips and a pickle. Her stomach grumbled loudly.

After wolfing down one big bite, Amber got the bottle together. She fetched a baby blanket and joined Noel.

The second June saw the bottle, she wanted it. "Baba ba ba."

Amber handed it to her, spread the blanket on the floor, then scooped June out of the playpen. She laid her down—but June didn't stay down.

Noel, she noticed, now stood across the room. "What," Amber asked, "do you think is going to happen?"

"I don't know."

While she wrestled with the baby, Amber grumbled "Coward" to him. But it was all she could do not to laugh.

He chewed his upper lip, ran a hand over his face, then came down to his knees beside her.

June stopped fighting. She held the bottle with one hand, and with the other she reached out. Noel offered her a finger and she grabbed it, then turned her big blue eyes on Amber.

She still looked sleepy, poor baby.

As she finished the diaper change, Amber said, "Thanks for the sandwich."

"You're welcome." He touched June's hair. "What does she eat?"

"Just about anything now, but she's partial to pasta." Amber scooped her up.

June didn't let go of Noel, so he got tugged along to

the kitchen. If he wanted to leave, Amber decided, he could say so. She wouldn't keep trying to spare him. She was many things, but a martyr wasn't one of them.

When she pulled the high chair around, he caught on and removed the tray for her, watching closely as she got June fastened in.

They made a good team, if only he'd realize it.

"You're good at all that," he said. "The diaper and bottle and this." He waved his free hand at the chair.

"I've always adored kids." She'd never planned on having one prior to love and marriage, but she'd adapt.

Noel looked away. "Want me to get you something to drink?"

"June Bug has you leashed," she said, glancing at the finger the baby gripped. "I'll get it." She also got food for June, which included a banana and a few pieces of the grilled cheese sandwich Noel had made for her.

"That's a gross combo."

She almost said, *Get used to it*, but edited that automatic reply at the last minute. Tonight could be the last she'd see Noel, at least in a domestic setting like this. Given he was a firefighter with her brother, running into him was unavoidable.

But again, she wouldn't think about that yet.

"I've seen her eat peas and peanut-butter toast, macaroni and apples, mashed potatoes and pickles. She likes most everything, but the combos are weird."

They ate in relative silence except for June's occasional babbling and antics that made them both chuckle.

It was all Amber could do to keep her eyes open.

Soon, June had the same problem. It amazed her how the little girl could simply fade out. Noel's finger was freed just in time for him to keep June from slumping over.

"She's out," Amber whispered. Without too much fuss, she cleaned June's hands and mouth, got her from the high chair and started toward the bedroom.

Noel stopped her. "Why don't you put her in the playpen? Then you can dry your hair without waking her."

"I won't be able to hear her."

He gave her a long, level look. "I'm staying, and my ears work just fine."

For a man who didn't like kids, he had an odd game plan. "You're sure about this?"

He nodded, then cleared the playpen, removing all but one stuffed animal.

After she'd settled the baby, she hastily retreated down the hall and into the bathroom, where she quietly closed the door.

This time she didn't get sidetracked with emotion, so she finished her hair a lot quicker than she had her shower. When she returned to the room, she found Noel on the floor beside the crib, on his back with his arms folded behind his head.

He appeared to be asleep, but she wasn't sure.

With a peek into the kitchen, she saw that he'd tidied up. The table was cleared and the high chair cleaned.

Lethargy dragged at her.

The house was so quiet. "Noel?" she whispered, but he didn't reply.

Slumping onto the sofa, she looked at him, so tall and fit, and then her gaze moved to the baby. Blast it, she was a goner. She could tell herself a million times that she'd make the adjustment without a hitch. But it was a lie.

Getting a baby was one thing.

Losing Noel was another.

CHAPTER FOUR

ONCE IN THE middle of the night, June awoke. She didn't fuss overly, and Noel was able to walk her around the house until she drifted off again.

But he couldn't hold her away from him without her protesting.

Fearing she'd wake Amber, he finally drew her close to his chest. Snuggling in, the baby idly touched his jaw, sleepily exploring his face. At one point she got her tiny fingers inside the neck of his shirt, tangling them in his chest hair. When she tugged, he quickly readjusted her. Little by little, her big blue eyes went drowsy and finally closed. Trustingly, her body went limp, her head slumped over his arm.

So tiny, he thought, studying her parted lips, the teensy button nose, the long lashes and round, rosy cheeks. She was so soft and she smelled indescribably good. Carefully, Noel touched his nose to her hair.

When he thought of what she'd lost, he wanted to hold her close and promise her everything would be okay. But she had Amber, and knowing Amber as he did, he trusted that she'd somehow make it okay.

His gaze shifted to where she'd passed out on the couch. She was every bit as boneless as June Bug.

Earlier when she'd whispered his name, he'd played

possum. He didn't want to leave her and figured she wouldn't wake him.

Yet he hadn't slept. Instead, on every level, he'd been aware of her, the quietness of her barefoot walk, the heat of her cobalt gaze, that iron will to do what she could, the best that she could, regardless of the odds or obstructions.

He didn't need Amber to give him the nitty-gritty details to know what had happened.

She'd been a rock.

He imagined the grief of Peggy's parents, and without a single doubt he knew Amber had shouldered as much as she could to spare them.

She would have given comfort, but had she received any?

Amber wasn't a woman to give in to tears…except that she *had* cried in the shower. Her puffy eyes proved it.

That had to mean she trusted him, and at the moment, her trust felt like an enormous gift.

At the very least, he could be here for her now to help with the transition. Tomorrow she'd have her whole family pitching in.

How would Rookie feel about a baby? Given the size of Amber's family, he already knew that the dog loved kids, but he was used to it just being him and Amber at home.

Wondering about it, Noel gently returned June to the playpen.

Amber hadn't stirred.

Maybe, his thoughts continued, that was where he could help out, spending more time with the dog, taking him to the park and for walks so Rookie could gradually get used to June. That'd take him away from her family's prying eyes, and also keep him out of contact with the baby.

Curled up on her side at one end of the couch, using the armrest like a pillow, Amber had drawn her long legs close to her chest. It was a protective posture, one that showed a vulnerability she'd never share while awake.

Dark, silky hair spilled everywhere, hiding her face. Her hands utterly lax. He could hear her deep, even breathing.

The urge to stretch out next to her burned hot inside him, but lust was the last thing she wanted or needed from him, and he couldn't hold her without wanting her. Instead he carefully placed a throw over her legs, then situated himself on the other end of the couch. He'd hear the baby if she awoke so he could get her again, giving Amber a chance to catch up on her sleep.

Wishing there was more he could do, wishing, even, that kids were in his future, he closed his eyes and tried not to think about tomorrow.

Nothing disturbed him until the knock on the door, and that jarred his eyes wide-open.

Noel realized several things at once.

June was standing in her playpen, looking at him.

The sun shone brightly through the windows.

And Amber was now tucked tightly to his side.

He lifted his head and looked toward the door. June said, "Up, up," with demand, her arms in the air.

Sleep cleared away in a rush.

Touching Amber's shoulder, he woke her. "Honey, you have company."

"Mm-mmm," she mumbled and burrowed closer.

God, that felt good. If only he'd awakened half an hour ago, he could have enjoyed it more. He kissed her forehead. "June Bug's awake."

At that, she lifted her head. She had one slim leg over his body, her knee resting on his crotch, and her breasts were firm against his ribs. Her hair trailed over his chest and shoulder and she blinked sleepy eyes. "What time is it?"

Scorched with sudden awareness, he croaked, "No idea."

Groaning, she sat up and looked at him. At all of him. In minute detail. After her gaze rose to meet his, she did her own croaking. "What are you doing here?"

Nice to know she wasn't immune, either. At least that hadn't changed. "I stayed over." He, too, sat up—and June repeated her demand to be held.

The knock came again.

"Oh my gosh." Amber was off the couch in a heartbeat, then she looked around as if trying to get her bearings. "Um…"

"I'll put on coffee," he said, trying to be helpful.

"Yes. Coffee." Since June wasn't fussing, Amber went to the door and swung it open.

Garrett stood there, his hand raised to knock. "Did I wake you?"

"I'm sorry, yeah. I overslept."

His gaze went past her and locked on Noel as he straightened the throw on the couch.

Thinking it wise to remove himself, Noel tried to make a run to the kitchen, but June wasn't having it. "Ma ma da."

Garrett's face split into a gentle smile. "Aw, she's adorable, sis." He hugged Amber and stepped in. "The folks are right behind me. Go do whatever you have to do and I'll see to the baby."

"Thanks."

Thanks? Noel frowned at her. She'd fought him every time he'd offered, but now with her brother—

"Try to look less like you spent the night, okay?" Garrett smirked at him. "Unless you want Dad to grill you all day."

Frowning, Noel ran both hands through his hair. "I was going to make coffee."

June reached toward him again.

Garrett scooped her up. "Hello, squirt. Aren't you a beauty?"

Rearing back, June studied him, looked to Noel, then back again. Her bottom lip started to quiver.

Automatically, Noel stepped forward. "She doesn't know you."

"And she knows you?"

"No, but..." He quickly realized Garrett didn't need any help.

"Shh, shh. It's okay, sweetheart." He held June close and rocked her a little. "We'll follow Noel, okay?" As he prodded Noel toward the kitchen, Garrett asked, "Where are the diapers? A bottle?"

Noel got those things for him, which Garrett utilized like an expert, and by the time he had the coffee going, Amber had returned.

She still looked sleep-sexy, but he tried not to notice. "Mind if I shave real quick?"

Her brows shot up. "Why would I mind?"

"Because I'll be using your razor."

She opened her mouth, glanced at her brother, then closed it again.

Garrett laughed.

Stepping closer and lowering her voice, Amber whispered, "Go home, Noel. You look as beat as I am and—"

He gave her a quick, firm smooch. "I told you I had the day off." As he walked away from her, he added, "I'll be back in five."

Noel wasn't sure what he was doing. He just knew he wasn't ready yet to leave her. Where was Rookie? He had assumed that Garrett had the dog.

By the time he'd shaved, gargled and finger-combed his hair, more family had arrived. He heard the noise before he reached the kitchen.

Rookie was there now and he raced to Noel to greet him, then looked toward the baby with unbridled excitement. Misty sat on the floor with June, Morgan next to her. Six feet from reaching them, Rookie lowered down to his stomach and army-crawled the rest of the way, his tail going wild. June laughed with delight—until she saw Noel.

Then she pushed away from Misty and came tottering to him in an animated, lopsided walk. When she reached him she lifted her arms. "Up."

"You must've done something right," Morgan said. "She likes you."

"No idea," Noel replied honestly. He glanced toward the kitchen to see Amber at the table talking to Garrett, who was cooking breakfast at the stove.

Now with her face scrunched up, June insisted, "Up!"

Laughing, Morgan scooped her up—and handed her to Noel.

When the baby grabbed him, Noel had no choice

but to take her. June put her hands to either side of his face and said, "Dug."

Wow! "Did you hear that?" He scanned the faces of Morgan and Misty. "She said *dog*."

"Dug." Then June clicked her tongue and Rookie came charging over.

"So clever," Misty said, joining her husband and Noel in the kitchen doorway.

Was she ever! Noel looked in the kitchen. "Amber, she said *dog*."

Amber gave him a curious glance, as if she'd never seen him before. "She's smart. I think there are about twenty words she knows."

And so the morning went.

Other family stopped in to visit, some for only a short time on their way to work, others for an hour or more. The men were every bit as enamored of June as the ladies were.

They were all more comfortable with her than Noel was.

Anytime Amber looked at him, she seemed oddly speculative, but with her family she was her usual, enthusiastic self.

Out of everyone there, June clearly preferred him, but she did let the others hold her. She just wasn't as relaxed with them.

They had breakfast together, and Noel made a point of sitting opposite the baby instead of right next to her. Amber, too, gave up her spot since Morgan and Misty were totally enthralled and wanted to get to know June better.

All the eggs and bacon were about gone when Misty said, "I can babysit while you work."

"Thanks, Mom, but I thought about it and decided I should set a routine right now. She's already had so many changes. I think it'll be better if I just pick up another playpen for the bookstore so I can take her with me." She looked at June with a smile. "I wouldn't mind the occasional sitter, though, once she gets used to everything."

Noel didn't say it, but he knew Amber preferred a leisurely bath over a quick shower. She also enjoyed long walks in the park with Rookie. Both would be more difficult with a fast-moving toddler to care for.

"How'd she do last night?" Morgan asked.

Amber turned a pointed look on Noel. "Ask him. I assume he got up with her, because once I crashed on the couch I didn't hear anything."

All eyes turned to Noel. He swallowed his last bite of toast and choked. While he was trying to get air back into his lungs, Garrett refilled his glass with orange juice.

They all waited until he could speak again.

Preferring a quick reply over detail, he rasped, "She was fine."

Unfortunately, that short answer didn't appease anyone.

Morgan sat back in his chair. "She slept through the night?"

"No, but she only woke up once."

"And?" Misty prompted.

"And..." What did they want to know? That he'd found something special in holding that tiny body close? That June had tugged on his heartstrings without even trying? That being near a baby complicated things he'd thought long settled? Not about to share his innermost turmoil, Noel shook his head. "And I walked with her a little."

"Where?" Garrett asked.

"Just around the house."

"I used to do that with my kids," Morgan said. "One or two trips through the house and they'd be out again. It gave Misty a chance to rest a little longer."

"Luckily," Misty said, "there were a few years between them, so by the time Garrett was born, Amber was a regular little helper."

"She's always been great with kids," Morgan said, and he beamed at his only daughter, then said to Noel, "You must be a natural, too."

He thought of his uncertainty over the bottle and diaper changing, and how easily Garrett and Amber had handled both. They were naturals. But him? "No," Noel assured them with stark honesty. "I'm not."

They paid no attention to his denial, continuing to ask questions intermixed with Morgan reminiscing about Amber as a baby.

Amber was the only one not talking, and she spent her time studying him. "June didn't need her diaper changed or anything. I think she just wanted to be held."

"That often does the trick," Misty said. "They're not little for long, so you need to soak up every minute that you can."

Wait...*what*? He hadn't been "soaking up" anything. His sole purpose had been to give Amber a break. "Actually, I—"

"Starting today," Amber cut in, taking the spotlight off him, "I'm going to work on getting her back to her routine." She spoke only to her family, not Noel.

Deliberately excluding him? Fine. The less involvement he had with little June Bug, the easier it'd be for him.

Not that he'd pay any attention to a dismissal. Amber should know him better than that by now. He'd still be around for her. But the baby…

"Was she on a schedule?" Misty asked.

"June's grandparents knew the timing of her naps and meals and bath. I'm hoping to stick with that."

Reaching out, Misty took her daughter's hand. "Don't pressure yourself or her too much, honey. Not just yet. It might take a bit of time before she settles in."

"But she *will* settle in," Morgan promised. "Kids are resilient."

Garrett put his hand on her shoulder. "Especially when they get unconditional love."

Yes, Noel thought, feeling like an interloper. Amber would give June that, and more.

Another knock sounded at the door, and as Rookie barked in excitement, additional family filed in. Watching the dog run off, June's eyes widened, she kicked her legs and clicked her tongue.

Rookie jerked to a halt and immediately skittered back to her side.

June would soon be a handful. Noel grinned, imagining it.

Then he caught Amber's appraising stare and quickly wiped the amusement off his face.

Shohn and Adam, the latest to show up, spent a few minutes playing with the baby. She appeared to adore everyone, but she also kept Noel in her sights.

They were all so good with kids. So comfortable.

He probably should go now. At this point he was just in the way, sort of hanging around on the outside. Not like he'd get any alone time with Amber now anyway. She had all the help she could need.

Shohn asked what they could do.

"How much time do you have?"

Adam said, "I'm free all day. Shohn has until two."

"Well," Amber said, "since it's only ten, there is something, if it wouldn't be too much trouble for you." Still she didn't look at Noel. "Peggy's parents gave me her minivan. It's ten years old, but runs well, and it really will be easier with the car seat. But obviously I couldn't drive home two vehicles yesterday. Do you think you could—"

"Give us directions and we're on it," Adam promised.

Amber headed to her purse on the counter to get her phone. "June has some other toys, too, and a swing set."

She continued to move at Mach speed, and Noel stood there, dazed at her renewed energy.

In every way that counted, Amber was now a mother. How was he supposed to get used to that? Then he looked at little June Bug and smiled at the way she flirted with Shohn and Adam.

"Let me call first to make sure it's okay." Amber stepped toward the window to use her cell.

Just then June made it clear that she wanted out of the high chair. Shohn got her down, and as soon as her tiny feet touched the floor, she came to Noel. "Up, up."

This time he picked her up without thinking about it too much. He even propped her against his side, the way he'd seen the others do. It was more comfortable for both of them.

June didn't weigh much, and she helped by holding on. Tightly.

When Amber finished her call, she wrote down

the address for Shohn, who planned to put it into his phone's GPS.

"Everything will be ready by the time you get there." She followed them to the door as they left, but Morgan, Misty and Garrett remained.

Noel watched her return to her seat, going past him with no acknowledgment at all.

"Amber?"

After an obvious hesitation, she lifted her gaze, taking in the way June rested against his shoulder. Some vague emotion crossed her face, possibly...yearning?

"Hmm?"

Noel had planned to make his excuses and head home, but what he said instead was "Mind if I go around and baby-proof the house?"

Amber cocked a brow.

Undeterred, he clarified, "Or at least see what you'll need for baby-proofing?" Kids were so easily hurt. Sometimes you couldn't take enough precautions. As a firefighter, he knew it only too well.

Shoving that thought away real quick, he waited on her answer.

She took her own sweet time thinking about it, her expression somehow speculative before finally giving him a big, beautiful smile. "She's getting around so well, it's a good idea."

His tension eased. "That's what I thought." Glad to have something to do, he started to turn.

"She's lucky to have you looking out for her."

Startled by that conclusion, he swung back around, making June laugh.

Smug over his reaction, Amber grinned. "I'm sure June appreciates it."

"I'm not—" Not what? Trying to ensure she didn't get hurt? Okay, he was. But mostly he'd just wanted some way to help out. For Amber.

June bounced in his arms, wanting him to swing her again…and he did, smiling as she squealed.

Until he realized her whole blasted family watched him. He shifted under their collective regard. "I'll go ahead and get started. Until it's done, keeping her in the playpen or holding her would be a good idea."

Garrett saved him from his own ramblings. "I taught that community class on safety in the home, so I'll help. You can start in here and I'll check out the bedrooms."

"Sounds good." Noel tried to hand June over, but she clung like a monkey, so rather than make an issue of it, he carried her with him while he inspected everything.

Rookie, who was still fascinated with the baby, followed along, stopping when they stopped, moving when they moved, always keeping his eyes on June. In between checking things and cuddling June, Noel gave the dog pats and praised him for being so diligent.

The cords for her lamps were a problem, but that could be solved by moving the couch against a wall. It wouldn't be ideal seating, but it'd be safer. Other plugs needed covers. The coffee table had some wicked corners. She'd need drawer guards, so little fingers couldn't get into everything.

Stepping around the dog, he made mental notes, and every so often June poked his face, pinched his ear, gently touched his eyelashes. Without thinking about it, Noel paused by the blind pulls and said, "Eye."

She touched her own and said "Eeeye" in an adorably exaggerated way.

Amazed, he shifted her around in front of him. "Nose?"

She touched his first, then her own and said with satisfaction, her voice going comically deep, "Nose."

His grin twitched. "What about an ear?"

She tickled his, laughing, and when he returned the favor, she squealed. That had Rookie barking in excitement again.

Noel sat down on the floor with her. Patting the space beside him, he invited Rookie to join in, then looked at June. "What else do you know, squirt?"

She grabbed his nose and said, "Honk."

He touched hers with one fingertip and said, "Beep."

They were both laughing, Rookie wiggling around them, when Amber came in to watch, her gaze transfixed.

Put on the spot, Noel said defensively, "She knows… things."

"Yes, she does. Most babies are fascinating little creatures."

He should have been more embarrassed, but damn it, he wanted to share, so he said, "Watch." He turned to June. "Where's your belly?"

She pulled up her T-shirt to show him, giggling when he tickled her. Amber smiled and came closer.

"June, where's your mouth?"

She opened wide. "Muf."

Amber knelt down and stroked Rookie. "Dog?"

"Dug." After saying it, she grinned so big she scrunched her whole face.

Utterly charmed, Noel hugged her small body to his chest before he thought better of it. June liked that enough to bounce hard—and the top of her head cracked the bridge of his nose.

"Ow, damn," he muttered, moving the baby back while squeezing the throbbing bridge of his nose.

June stared at him. "Dim."

He froze. "Um, no, honey. That's not a nice word. I shouldn't have—"

"Dim!"

Amber snickered.

"It's not funny."

"Your eyes are watering," Amber pointed out needlessly.

Because she'd caught him good. "At least she didn't hurt her head."

"Dim."

Noel groaned.

From the doorway, Morgan said, "I slipped up all the time. You'll get used to it."

That took the humor right out of Amber. She stood, saying to June, "Let's let Noel finish up, sugar, okay?"

Grabbing Noel, the baby chanted, "Dim, dim, dim!"

"Oh Lord," Noel grumbled, even as he lifted her into his arms. "It's okay. I don't mind."

Amber threw up her hands and stalked off.

She didn't *want* him to get used to it; she'd made that clear enough.

But then, he didn't want to, either…right? He held June back and looked at her.

She grinned.

No kids, ever. He'd spelled it out for Amber and hadn't yet said anything to the contrary. At the time, he hadn't known…couldn't have guessed…

What? That he'd be overwhelmed with feelings for a baby he didn't even know?

June leaned in to put a wet kiss on his cheek, and damned if his heart didn't melt a little.

After giving him a pitying look, Rookie went after Amber.

Morgan, his gaze knowing, said, "Make me a list and I'll go to the store."

"Sure." Though he'd planned to do that himself, he wouldn't mind handing it off to her dad since he wasn't quite ready to go.

"You're so good with June Bug, it'd be better if you hung around for the day."

From the kitchen, Amber complained, "Dad!"

Morgan only grinned, waiting, his back to his daughter.

Showing his never-before-known fickle nature, Noel rubbed the baby's back and agreed. "Sure. I'll stick around."

He heard a thump.

Grin widening, Morgan whispered, "That was probably Amber's head. Sometimes she doesn't know what's good for her." Without waiting for Noel to react to that, he turned and said, "Misty, you want to come along? You can help me pick out what we need."

Amber groused, "I can get the stuff myself, Dad. Having a baby doesn't make me helpless."

"I know, honey. But I'm a grandpa now, so don't deprive me of my fun."

While holding June, dodging her hands as she tried to grab the pen, Noel made his list, then gave it to Garrett so he could add his suggestions. For the time being everyone decided it was best to keep all doors closed so June couldn't get into the bedroom or bathroom.

Morgan and Misty left.

Garrett offered to take June and Rookie into the backyard to play so Amber could tell Noel how to rearrange her furniture.

Reluctantly, Noel shifted the little girl into Garrett's arms. She looked uncertain about it, but then Garrett pretended to chew on her belly and she ended up laughing and pulling his hair. Since Rookie wanted out, June went willingly, too.

Noel stood there, waiting, until Amber came out of the kitchen to join him.

Her long hair hung loose today, dark as midnight, so silky smooth it appeared liquid. She didn't wear any makeup, but with her dark arched brows and thick inky lashes, she didn't need it.

She'd dressed in another loose T-shirt and slim jeans—no shoes, and he was pretty sure no bra.

The longer he looked at her, the harder his heart thumped.

For her part, she studied the furniture with single-minded purpose.

Noel moved closer to her. "If I can make some suggestions?"

She stated, "The couch should go there."

He touched her cheek. "No. It'd be better on the opposite wall."

Frowning, she nodded. "Fine. Then we could put the bookcase there."

Slowly, Noel curved his hand around her nape. "The bookcase should be moved into your bedroom. There are too many breakable things on it, and it could tip over if she pulls up on one of the shelves."

"Right." With a deep sigh, she tossed up her hands. "Babysitting for a few hours is one thing. I handled that, piece of cake. Setting up house with a toddler in mind is altogether different. I don't know what I'm doing."

"Wrong." Cautiously, Noel drew her against him. "You're loving her. That's the most important thing." He might not know a lot about kids, but he knew that with a certainty.

"She's lost so much."

"True. But you're doing everything you can. I'd say that's enough."

Amber gave in, wrapping her arms around him. "Okay, so we know what I'm doing. What are *you* doing?" She tipped her head back to lock gazes with him. "You don't have to be here, you know."

He brushed his fingertips along her temple, bent to lightly touch his mouth to hers and gave her the only truth he had. "You're here," he said. "Where else would I be?"

CHAPTER FIVE

AMBER DIDN'T KNOW what to think. From the moment she'd realized June would be hers, she'd decided to be straightforward with Noel. She'd have given a lot to have him share this with her. She definitely didn't want him to go.

She loved him.

But as a realist, she chose to face her future head-on, not waste time longing for things she couldn't have.

And so she'd explained to him—and yet, he hadn't left. If anything, he'd dug in deeper. Even more surprising, he was amazing with June.

His big hands moved up and down her back, each pass pressing her closer until she felt the strong beat of his heart. "You're confusing me."

"I know." He kissed her temple. "I'm sorry."

That was it? No further explanation? "You shouldn't be here. I assumed you wouldn't be."

"I'm worried about you."

Only worried? Amber tried to move away, but he didn't let her and she couldn't find the energy to make an issue of it. "You don't have to worry about me. You can see I'm fine, and I have plenty of help."

"You're holding it together," he agreed, "but then no one doubted you would. That doesn't mean you *shouldn't* grieve. In less than a week, you lost a close friend and took on an enormous responsibility."

Noel smelled so good, she wanted to stay right where she was, her nose against his throat, his strong arms around her. But that, too, was unrealistic, so she gave him the answers he needed, the answers that might free him.

"What you said is true, and I suppose if I wanted to concentrate on the struggles, I could. I'd be in tears in minutes and then what? What good would it do?" She hugged him, this beautiful, caring man she loved so much. "I'd rather concentrate on the idea that Peggy trusted me to raise her daughter for her. That's the most amazing compliment I've ever gotten. If I focus on the positive, on the fact that June wasn't in the car with her, that she has a long life ahead of her and I have a loving family who will ensure she's never alone, then I can deal with it more easily."

It would be so much easier if Noel would be part of her new life, but she couldn't force him to love her enough. She wouldn't even try.

She'd always wanted children, he clearly had not. It wouldn't be right for her dreams to overshadow his.

Noel touched her face so tenderly. Blast the man, it felt like love, like love strong enough to conquer anything.

"We need to talk," he said.

She couldn't imagine what else there was to say, but if that was what he needed, she'd happily agree. "Okay."

"Ah, babe, don't do that. You don't need to fake it with me."

She choked, remembering the first time he'd said that to her.

Noel nipped her bottom lip. "I thought we settled that early on."

"We did!" With her face hot, Amber scowled at him. The discussion at the time had been embarrassing enough. Okay, so she had faked it a little their first time together. Just a little because she didn't want him to think of her as too much work.

To her surprise, he'd somehow known and had set her straight real quick, saying he loved touching and tasting her, claiming he could spend hours enjoying her—then he'd proved it until she'd had an explosive climax.

Afterward he'd insisted that she always be honest with him, most especially in bed. "Your games," he'd said, "have no place here. Not between us."

Being honest with him had given her a big payoff, and somehow every time proved better than the last.

"That's not what we were talking about," she protested.

"But it applies. No matter the situation, you never need to put on a brave front for me." He cupped her face and put his mouth to hers, his lips coaxing hers apart, his tongue touching softly, then going deeper.

Throughout her life, she'd been able to resist any temptation that didn't suit her self-designed goals.

Except for Noel. She'd never been able to resist him.

He tilted his head to deepen the kiss even more. She felt his warm hand on the bare skin of her back, then pressing into her jeans to cover one plump cheek.

Amber gasped, not with surprise but with scorching need. She could really use an outlet right now, and she couldn't think of a better way to—

"Sorry," Noel murmured against her lips. "I didn't mean… That got out of hand."

Had he heard her complain? No, he hadn't. "It always does with you."

"I know." He crushed her close again. "It was supposed to be a kiss of understanding and support. I want you to know that you can lean on me. Cry if you need to. Rail at fate."

"Gee, that sounds really glum." She'd rather keep pushing forward than wallow in uncertainty.

Noel didn't smile. "Just be yourself, okay? That's all I'm saying. Whatever you're feeling or thinking, I want you to share with me."

"There's a problem with that offer." Why did she have to keep reminding him? "You," she said with a poke at his chest, "don't like kids."

Her exasperation didn't bother him. He caught her finger and held on. "That's one of the things I wanted to talk about." They both heard Garrett coming back in, forcing him to add, "But not until we're alone."

Alone now had an all-new connotation. The adults might vacate her house, but June would always be with her. And babies, she knew, could be most unpredictable.

As if he'd read her thoughts, he said, "Let me stay over again. I can leave early enough to go home and change before work."

"Noel—"

"I *need* to be with you, honey." He kept his voice soft, coaxing. "Let me stay."

Regardless of what was right in the long term, how could she refuse him when she so badly wanted to give in? Everyone might see her as a strong, capable woman, but around Noel, she was mush—and he knew it. "Okay, fine. Suit yourself."

He kissed her one more time. "I love you, too, you know. Don't forget that."

Her eyes flared at that never-before-heard sentiment, but before she could properly react, Garrett, June and Rookie reentered with a whirlwind of fun chaos and she lost the opportunity.

For now.

JUNE BUG WENT straight to Noel, of course. That, Amber decided, was another problem. How could she let the baby get so attached to him if he might suddenly bail?

But he said he loved her.

"Come along, little sister." Garrett pulled her into the kitchen.

"What's going on?"

"You tell me. Something's up with you and Noel—and don't tell me it's none of my business because one man can't ignore the misery of another."

"He might be miserable," she said, "but don't expect me to shed any light."

"Start there," Garrett insisted. "I'll figure it out as I go along."

Since she did need someone to talk to, Amber spilled the whole story. She kept an eye on the doorway and pitched her voice low, but she and Garrett both could hear Noel playing with June.

"And that's all of it," she said.

Both Garrett's brows went up. "He said he doesn't want kids, *ever*?"

"Yup. Of course, he didn't know anything about June at the time, but he was pretty convincing."

Noel's laugh came from the living room, then Rookie barked.

Garrett rolled his eyes. "Did you ask him why?"

"I would have, but then I got the call…"

"And then you got June." He shook his head. "Noel's not familiar with kids, anyone can see that."

"Just as anyone can see he's not immune?"

"Not even close. June already has his heart wrapped up. Talk to him, okay? Find out what his hang-up is with kids, and then the two of you can work it out."

Could it really be that easy?

Garrett frowned down at her. "I see the self-doubt. You're off your game or I wouldn't have had to give you this little pep talk. You'd have seen the obvious signs on your own."

"What signs?"

"That Noel cares, not just about you, but about a little girl he doesn't even know. When he moved here, I wondered why. He'd had a good position in Lexington, but he uprooted and came to our small town."

Amber thought about that. "He told me he just wanted a change. I never questioned that." She peeked at her brother. "We had other priorities whenever we were together."

"Noticed," Garrett said, "and we don't need to go into how you two mooned over each other."

"But thinking about it now, it does sound like a man running away." Frowning, Amber wondered aloud, "But from what?"

Garrett said, "Maybe you should find out."

Yes, she really should. Smiling, Amber threw herself into his arms. "I love you, little brother."

"Love you, too." He stood. "Now put that sharp brain

and conniving manner of yours to work and fix things, okay?"

She rubbed her hands together. "You know, I think I will."

IN SHORT ORDER, working together, her family got her house as baby-safe as it could be. Garrett screwed in all the drawer latches, Amber added rubber bumpers to every sharp corner, and Noel got her furniture rearranged in the way they'd decided on—which was basically the way he'd deemed best.

After Adam and Shohn returned with the minivan, Shohn, a park ranger, left for work. Garrett, too, had to go and Morgan had a meeting, but Misty stayed behind.

Adam and Noel got June's dresser set up while Misty put all her clothes away. A toy box went into the living room where the bookcase used to be. The swing set, made of thick plastic, went into the yard under the overhang.

All in all, they had it as together as they could in such a short time.

Misty ordered pizza and salads for dinner. Shortly after they ate, she hugged Amber, made her promise she'd call if she needed anything at all and, with a final kiss to June, she left. Adam, anxious to see his wife, Isabella, followed her lead, right down to the offer to help any way he could, then he, too, ended the visit.

Finally they were alone.

It would have been a good time to talk, but June was still so energetic, Noel couldn't see starting a deep conversation only to have it repeatedly interrupted with a toddler's antics.

Besides, he enjoyed her silly games and babbling.

Amber hoped a bath would help her unwind, so she got the tub ready while Noel kept an eye on June.

To keep her entertained, he went to his back and bench-pressed the baby, making silly noises at her each time he lowered her, then listening to her squeals as he lifted her high.

When Amber came to get June, she was laughing so hard that it got Amber laughing, too.

Noel smiled at the sound. Amber had every reason to be grim, but instead she took pleasure in life. She was an amazing woman in so many ways.

And she was his.

Rookie didn't know what to think. He constantly wanted to sniff and snuffle on June, but very, very gently.

Amber hesitated. "You could watch TV or something while I give her a bath. That is, if you still plan to stay."

"I'm staying." But Noel didn't want any distance between them. "How about I help with the bath?"

Those gorgeous blue eyes widened. "My bathroom is so small..."

"We'll fit." *Like a family.* The particular thought, like so many that he'd had today, warmed him. "Come on." If he gave her a chance, she'd cut him out again, and he wasn't about to let that happen.

Rookie wanted in the room, too. He sat beside the tub, resting his head on the edge, whining as if worried.

Amber had put June in a clever bathing seat that kept her from slipping.

Didn't keep her from splashing, though. The girl liked her water. She kicked and slapped and overall had such a great time that she soaked everyone, including the dog.

Just as Amber had suspected, though, by the time she was dried off and put in a T-shirt and clean diaper for bed, she had wound down considerably. Amber struggled to clean June's teeth with a small, soft toothbrush, then filled her bottle with water.

When she tried to sit down with June, the baby squirmed, her gaze searching for Noel.

She made her preference clear.

It surprised him, and secretly pleased him. Noel didn't mind holding her. Already it felt natural, more so than he'd ever suspected it could. Oddly, as the good feelings built up, they crowded out the bad ones. A few reservations remained, but they no longer felt so important.

June got comfortable in his lap with her head in the crook of his arm so she could see both of them. She held her bottle with one hand, and with the other, she grasped a small fistful of Noel's T-shirt.

He stroked her hair as her eyes grew heavier. Amber turned the TV on for background noise, to help drown out other sounds, like Rookie's thumping tail as he watched the baby fall asleep.

The second she was out, Rookie gave up his vigil with a big yawn and padded over to the corner to flop down into his doggy bed.

Noel turned to Amber. She appeared relaxed, her head resting back, her gaze on June.

"Today was nice," he said in a low whisper. "I hadn't expected that."

Her gaze sought his. "You expected misery being around a child?"

"Not misery, no. But I didn't expect fun."

Rather than question his meaning, she nodded. "I enjoyed it, too...and I feel a little guilty about it, knowing what Peggy will miss."

He reached out to lace his fingers with hers. "That's understandable. But I like your idea of focusing on what's right instead of what's wrong." He lifted her hand and kissed her knuckles. "Peggy knew how you'd be or she wouldn't have chosen you. I guarantee you she doesn't want you miserable. That'd only make June Bug miserable, too."

"Maybe." She gave it some thought, then twisted to face him more. "Since we're about as alone now as we're going to get, can I tell you something? Something very private?"

He searched her face, but didn't find a clue what this could be about. "You can tell me anything." As long as she didn't tell him to leave. With an odd possessiveness, he curled June Bug a little closer.

"You're sure? Because it's a biggie."

Uneasiness stirred. "Anything," he promised, looking at their entwined hands.

Silence stretched out. The low sounds of the television faded.

And Amber said, "I'm illegitimate."

NOT SURPRISINGLY, Noel's dark gaze swung to hers. "What?"

"Dad isn't really my dad. I mean, he is, at least in all the most important ways. But he didn't father me. My mother was already pregnant when she met him."

Bemused, Noel looked at each of her features, then shook his head. "But you look like him."

"I look like Mom. It just happens that they both have dark hair and blue eyes." She smiled thinking about it.

"It never mattered to Dad. He knew Mom was pregnant shortly after he met her, but he fell in love and that was that. When I was born, he made it clear to one and all that I *am* his daughter."

"How did you find out?"

Her mouth twisted. "I overheard Mom and Dad talking once when they didn't know I was around. Mom was laughing about how I have Dad's mannerisms and she told him he was such a wonderful father than no one would ever know I wasn't really his. When they saw me, Dad was wrecked, but Mom just explained everything."

"How old were you?"

"Fifteen. Plenty old enough to understand and to realize that my daddy adored me. Nothing else mattered."

Noel just whispered, "No, nothing else matters."

"Family knows, but not anyone else."

"Except me?"

She touched his chest. "Well, you're like family, right? Especially after taking care of June all day."

She held her breath, waiting to see how Noel would take that. It pleased her when he smiled.

"My point," she said, "is that it doesn't matter to me who birthed June Bug. Yes, I'll tell her all about her mother. I'll make sure she knows what a wonderful person Peggy was and how much she loved her. But June is mine now and she'll stay mine and that's never going to change."

"I didn't think it would. Give me credit for knowing you better than that, okay?" Very carefully, he stood and started down the hall with the baby to put her to bed.

Feeling like an anxious new mom, Amber waited only a moment before following. She got to the doorway in time to see Noel brush a kiss over June's forehead then lower her to the mattress.

Rookie sauntered in around her, headed underneath the crib and curled up to sleep with a big doggy sigh.

There seemed to be so many beautiful moments to make her overly emotional. Noel's affection for June, Rookie's protectiveness.

Noticing that Noel wasn't as adept at raising the side rail, she stepped in and, showing him how it worked, did it for him so he wouldn't wake June.

Of course, he'd just put the baby in the crib…right next to her bed. Sex was out, then. "If you'd given me a chance, I'd have suggested the playpen."

"You said you were getting her routine under way today. I figured that meant the crib."

Bummed that he'd be so blasé about it, she took his hand and said, "Come on." She had a few things to say to him.

When she reached the living room, she turned to face him…and forgot what she'd planned to say.

He stared down at her like a starving man.

"Noel?"

"I know you're exhausted," he explained.

"Not really."

As if she hadn't spoken, he continued with "And I know you have your mind on a million things other than sex."

"Not so." Given the heat in his eyes, sexual satisfaction had just jumped way up on her list.

"I shouldn't be thinking about—"

With a grumbling sigh, Amber went on tiptoe and put her lips to his firm mouth. She breathed in a heady dose of his irresistible scent, curling her toes in pleasure.

Fisting her hands in his shirt, she said, "Listen up, Noel. I want you. Right now. But June could wake up any second."

"I understand."

"So," she said, stressing the word since he'd interrupted again, "you need to talk less and touch more. Got it?"

His mouth curled in a sensual smile. "Yeah, I think I do." With that said, he scooped her up, took two steps to the couch and went down with her under him.

CHAPTER SIX

AT THAT PARTICULAR moment, Noel wouldn't have cared if they were on the floor, or standing against the wall, or hell, with her bent over a table.

That last one enticed him and he considered it.

He needed her bad, the feel of her skin against his, the touch of her small hands, the warmth of her body as it cradled his…

Their last aborted effort to get intimate had been followed by a long separation and then a foundation-shaking surprise, leaving him in extended want. She'd left him primed and now it felt like he'd suffered long-term foreplay. He'd been spinning since her return, and yet, the craving for her remained. Add in all the unfamiliar heart-tugging emotions, and he could barely think past the desire to claim her again, to make sure she understood that they belonged together.

Holding her head between both hands, he feasted on her mouth, loving the softness of her lips, the damp stroke of her tongue, the mewling sounds of pleasure. While he kissed her, she writhed under him, trying to hurry him along, robbing him of patience.

The second he moved from her mouth to her throat, she gasped with desperation, "We're on a timetable here, Noel!"

"I know." June could wake, but still, he wanted to

relish every part of this, a new beginning—whether she realized it or not. "I need everything, honey."

She went still, then her hands clenched in his hair to lift his face. "Everything?"

Heat flushed her cheeks and made her blue eyes bright. Her lips were swollen. "Everything you have to give." He took her mouth again, distracting her while he unsnapped and unzipped her jeans, then worked a hand up inside her shirt, coasting his palm along the dip of her waist, her ribs, until he closed a hand over one plump, warm breast.

Against his palm, her nipple tightened. He caught it between finger and thumb, tugging gently, rolling—

"Noel."

Lowering himself, he shoved the shirt up to her chin, plumped one breast in his hand and latched on to her, sucking strongly.

With a harsh groan, she lifted her hips against him, seeking closer contact.

He'd missed this so much. Her excitement, the combustible chemistry, her scent, and the feel of her hair and skin.

He'd missed *her.*

He was a different man with Amber. A better man, happier, more complete.

Sitting up in a rush, Noel whisked the shirt off over her head, then removed his own.

As he stood to kick off his shoes and strip off his jeans, she struggled to remove her own. Once he was naked, Noel tried to help her, but he got distracted with her body and bent to kiss the delicate curve of her belly, each sleek thigh as they were revealed.

"Noel," she complained, her voice high and thin with need. "If we get interrupted, I'll die."

"Shh." He tugged her jeans away, then her minuscule panties, dropping them both to the floor. "I'll take care of you." He touched her sex, lightly stroking, then dipped his head to nuzzle against her, savoring the musk of her excitement. Her silken thighs opened wider. He helped her with that, lifting one leg to the back of the couch, moving the other over the side until her foot rested on the floor.

Using both hands, he kept her open as he looked at her. Then he had to touch again. And taste.

Blue eyes ablaze, arms reaching for him, Amber whispered, "I need you now."

He saw that she did, but he wanted her pleasure first. If the baby awoke and one of them had to suffer frustration, he'd rather it be him.

"Soon," he replied and bent back to her. "Now try not to make too much noise."

Knowing what would come, she moaned harshly, then snatched a throw pillow to hold over her face.

While he nibbled and licked, he plied one fingertip over her swollen lips. With each touch she got wetter—and he stroked deeper until he had two fingers firmly pressed inside her. She couldn't hold still, so he drew her swollen clitoris into his mouth and suckled ever so softly.

Just as he'd known she would, Amber came apart within minutes, her hips riding rhythmically against his mouth, her cries harsh and real but, thankfully, muffled under the pillow.

Her entire body went taut, her thighs trembling while she ground out a much-needed climax.

As her arms fell away and her legs went utterly lax, sprawling even more, Noel moved up over her body and removed the pillow. Smiling from the inside out, he asked, "You okay, sweetheart?"

Feathery black lashes rested over damp cheekbones. Her parted lips drew slow, deep breaths. He felt her heartbeat thundering against his chest.

Finally she managed a slight nod.

Amber was always beautiful, but in his opinion, never more so than right after release. "Listen."

She got her heavy eyes to open the tiniest bit. "To what?"

"Silence, meaning June is still sleeping, so now it's my turn." He brushed his mouth over hers. "But I wouldn't mind if you joined me."

She got her eyes open more. "I don't know if I—"

He slid deep, cutting off whatever she would have said. Wet, hot, with little aftershocks from her release that squeezed him. Keeping a slow and easy rhythm wasn't easy. Before he lost control, he framed her face in his hands. "I love you, Amber Hudson." Saying it affected him and he thrust harder.

She tipped back her head in pleasure. "I love you, too," she managed on a gasp.

"I know." He watched her as he quickened his pace. "Put your legs around me."

It required two shuddering breaths before she said, "I still have legs?"

Amazing that she could amuse him in the middle of lust. "Yeah. Sexy legs—like the rest of you."

"You make me feel sexy." She got her arms around his neck first, then locked her ankles over the small of his back. "Better?"

Noel couldn't speak. The position took him so deep, he felt a part of her. Now. Forever.

When she quickened under him, he put his face in her neck and concentrated on waiting for her.

"Noel." She squeezed him tight as her climax built. *"Noel."*

As soon as she shattered, he let himself go and joined her, growling low in his throat as pleasure ripped through him.

Long minutes later, all his tension drained away, Noel argued with himself that he had to get up before he smothered her.

But not just yet.

Her fingertips trailed up and down his back and every so often she hugged him or pressed a kiss to his shoulder.

Finally she asked, her soft voice tentative, "Noel?"

"Hmm?"

"Are you sure you don't want to head home to get a good night's sleep?"

It took an effort, but he got up to his elbows so he could look into her eyes, now smoky blue in the aftermath of her release. "You really know how to destroy an ego, don't you?"

She lightly touched her fingertips to his mouth. "Your ego is just fine and dandy."

"True enough." He lifted a little higher to look at her breasts. "I have beneath me the most beautiful, intelligent, caring woman in all of Buckhorn, maybe in all of Kentucky."

"Just Kentucky?"

He grinned and settled against her again, smoothing a palm over her hip. "I didn't want to spoil you with flattery."

"I'm spoiled with sexual satisfaction. What's a little flattery added in?"

"True." He lingered at her lips, unable to stop kissing her, but before he got carried away, he sat up. "With everything you have going on, you haven't forgotten birth control?"

"No." She sat up, too. "I want you all the time, no matter what else is happening, so how could I forget?"

Plus she knew how he supposedly felt about kids, and while Amber took joy in manipulating things as she saw fit, he knew she'd never involve a child.

She gathered up her shirt and panties. "Be right back."

Noel had so much to say to her, he impatiently pulled on his boxers and jeans, then paced. The talk wouldn't wait. It needed to be tonight. Tomorrow would no doubt be another hectic day with her family around.

In fact, a day rarely went by when she didn't see a few members of her family. With June Bug here now, he imagined the visits would ramp up. If he wanted any time alone with her, he needed to adjust their relationship.

And he would. Tonight.

Expression thoughtful, Amber strolled back in. She'd pulled on the clothes she'd taken with her and had her long, dark hair in a braid.

Noel caught her hand and pulled her into his lap on the couch. He smelled the toothpaste on her breath and knew she was ready for bed. "I know you're tired, and you need more sleep—"

"You slept less than I did last night."

He put a finger to her lips. "No arguing, not right now. It's my turn to tell you something."

"This sounds serious."

"I suppose it is." He drew her against him. Talking about it would be easier without her watching him. "I came to Buckhorn to escape. I needed time alone, away from the city."

She walked her fingers up his chest. "That time alone didn't last long."

"No. I saw you at the fire station when you came to visit Garrett and then happily let you chase me to ground."

"Hey." Laughing, she lightly punched him.

"You know you did." He kissed the top of her head. "And I'm glad. I realized shortly after meeting you that being alone gave me too much time to stew on things I had hoped to leave behind. Unfortunately, whether I stewed or not, it was there."

"It?"

He played with her braid while trying to get the words in order. "We got called out to a house fire one night. It was bad." Noel went over it in his mind, something he still did far too often, and decided the details weren't all that important, so he cut to the tragic ending. "An entire family died, including two small kids." His throat tightened and he had to take a minute before speaking again. "I carried them out, but it was already too late. The little boy made it to the hospital. I stayed with him while they tried to find relatives. But he didn't recover. By the next morning when an aunt had arrived, he was gone."

Saying nothing, Amber shifted to face him, her bent legs on either side of his hips, her arms locked around his neck, her head against his chest. She surrounded him with her love, holding him close.

Noel rested his cheek against the top of her head. "I don't have words for how devastating it was. Nothing has ever leveled me like that."

"I can't even imagine," she whispered, and he heard the tears in her voice.

"I made the hasty decision to never have kids. If losing a child I didn't know could hurt so badly, what would it be like if he were mine?"

Amber hugged him tighter. "I understand."

Being so intuitive, caring and kind, she probably did.

But he doubted she understood it all.

"I love you so much, Noel," she whispered. "I'd do just about anything for you. I hope you know that."

"I do."

"But June is mine now. I can't let her go. I wouldn't even want to."

"And that," he said, "is something I understand, because you're mine, and I can't, *won't*, let you go."

She faced him, her gaze searching.

"I've been a fool," he admitted. "When I made that ridiculous pledge to myself, I hadn't counted on meeting you. Or June. Or how holding a little girl would make me feel so many things, all of them good, filling me up so that the bad feelings barely had room left to stay."

Hope changed her expression. "What are you saying?"

"In less than a day, June won me over."

"She's been very sweet," Amber admitted. So far, June's adjustment had astounded everyone. But Noel, unused to children, might not realize that, so she felt she had to be up-front and honest. "There will be times when she's impossible. When she's sick and whiny, or having a temper tantrum. She's independent. She's bound to make demands. All kids do. It's all part of growing up, but regardless, she'll be mine."

As if he anticipated June's various moods, he smiled. "It already feels like she's mine, too."

With her mood guarded, Amber whispered, "She could be."

"And Rookie?"

A small smile blossomed. "He already adores you."

"Hell, you may as well know, I've already been thinking of your whole family as mine."

Amber put a shaky hand to her mouth. "You mean that?"

Touching her cheek, Noel moved his fingertips over her velvet skin. "They're part and parcel with you, honey, but more than that, they're good people. And they love you. How could I not love them for that?"

Tears dampened her lashes, but she was grinning. "So...we're in this together?"

"Richer or poorer, through sickness and health."

Her eyes flared, then she threw herself against him.

Noel smiled. "Will you marry me, Amber?"

Against his neck, she nodded. "I would have asked if you hadn't."

"I know."

She laughed.

"But while you're being agreeable..." He lowered a hand to her panty-covered bottom and pulled her closer to him. "We don't need two houses, right? So before June gets *too* settled here, how about we move to my house? I have a little more room, and I know you like the place since you helped me pick it. The yard is fenced.

I can put in a doggy door for Rookie that leads into the sunroom, instead of the kitchen, so June Bug won't discover it. And she'd have her own room. Plus—"

Amber kissed him.

He gave her a curious look when she sat back again. "Is that a yes?"

"That was me copying your methods for gaining silence." She grinned at him. "You don't have to sell me on the idea, Noel. I love you, my family loves you, and I've always known your house would be perfect for a family."

"So clever," he teased.

Her eyes sparkled with happiness. "How do you feel about a very small, not-very-formal wedding?"

"That's what you want?"

"I want you. I want us to be a family. Given the circumstances with June, I'd prefer fast over fancy—unless you want something more?"

"I only want you happy."

Just as they heard a cry that meant June had awoken, Amber whispered, "Consider it done."

THEY MADE THE transition easily. Everything that had just been done to Amber's house to baby-proof it got transferred to Noel's.

With all her family pitching in, the move and setup were accomplished in a single day.

His extra bedroom and bathroom made his house a little bigger, and Amber considered it the perfect size.

The wedding would happen at the end of July. In the meantime, she returned to work and took June with her.

Her first day back proved easier than she'd imagined. Buckhorn was a small town and everyone knew everyone else, meaning when she needed a moment to change June's diaper or feed her, any customers in the store were understanding. Some were even delighted.

June enjoyed the attention, and since her mama had worked, she was used to sitters. But the girl had a temper, and when she wanted Noel, she wanted him.

Amber understood that—because she felt the same.

It wasn't easy convincing June that she had to wait sometimes, like when he worked or had to shower, especially when Noel proved so accommodating. He'd bend over backward to give the little girl everything she wanted, including himself.

He'd gone from not wanting kids to doting on June's every whim.

It was over dinner one night that Amber watched him alternately eat and entertain June. She loved them both so much, there were times when it almost overwhelmed her. How could one woman be so happy?

"Thank you, Noel."

He glanced up from the steak he'd grilled while Amber, June and Rookie had played in the yard. "You cook as often as I do."

"I know, and I do thank you for dinner, but that's not what I meant."

"No?"

How to start? From the beginning, he'd been different from any person she'd known. "I didn't entirely control our relationship."

He laughed. "Not for lack of trying. But I figured out early on that you wouldn't accept a pushover. If I wanted you, and you can bet I did, I had to be different."

"So you made me work for it?"

He lifted his tea in a salute. "What better way to make you appreciate me, once you had me?"

"And I do," she agreed. "Being here with you and June, feeling so…complete. That's why I'm thanking you. I didn't plan all this, but turns out it's everything I ever wanted."

Noel smiled at her. "Everything? Because, see, in a year or two, a little longer if you need it, I was thinking another baby might be nice."

Her eyes rounded. "Another baby?" Then with a giant grin, "You mean it?"

After smiling at June, he set aside his fork to take Amber's hand. "I was so afraid to be around a kid, thinking it'd bring back that nightmare. Instead, you two have made me happier than I knew was possible. If you want five kids, I'm ready."

Amber laughed. "One or two is plenty for me, and waiting a while is a good idea." She leaned forward to kiss him.

Which had June complaining—until they each kissed her instead.

* * * * *

The Buckhorn Brothers—hot, protective and oh-so-alpha...especially around the women they love.

Don't miss any of the Buckhorn series, available now from Lori Foster and HQN Books!

BUCKHORN BEGINNINGS
(featuring Sawyer and Morgan)

FOREVER BUCKHORN
(featuring Gabe and Jordan)

THE BUCKHORN LEGACY
(featuring Casey)

BUCKHORN EVER AFTER
(Shohn and Nadine's story)

BACK TO BUCKHORN
(Garrett and Zoey's story)

A BUCKHORN SUMMER
(Lisa and Gray's story)

A BUCKHORN BACHELOR
(Adam and Isabella's story)

A BUCKHORN BACHELOR

To the Animal Adoption Foundation,
www.AAFPets.org.

Thank you for all you do
to help dogs and cats in need. I know
my contributions are always put to very good use.
It's been a true pleasure watching the AAF grow!

CHAPTER ONE

ADAM SOMMERVILLE STROLLED around the perimeter of the carnival, keeping watch on the kids and checking out the different games and rides while also steering clear of the clingier ladies. Being an almost-thirty-year-old bachelor from a leading family in a small town made him prime pickings. Even in the fun atmosphere of the carnival, the sunny June weather, and the crowds who'd turned out to support the elementary school, he wasn't safe from marriage-minded ladies. Especially when members of his own family conspired against him. Many of them figured it was past time for him to settle down.

How the hell had he gotten so old?

Thirty. The big three-oh.

He didn't feel thirty, yet. For sure he wasn't ready for it. Not that he obsessed on age or anything. He had a terrific life, a life he loved. He enjoyed being free and clear, taking on only those responsibilities of his choosing.

Like his insane, enormous, and awesome family.

Or his job as an elementary school gym teacher, which suited him perfectly.

But he had to admit, lately it felt like something was missing.

Maybe because he'd never planned to stay…alone.

Snorting at himself, Adam kept walking, trying to out-pace his thoughts. He wasn't *alone*, not in that maudlin, depressed way. He had a wealth of relatives, plenty of good friends, and whenever he needed it, he found female companionship.

Tonight seemed like one of those nights.

The oppressive heat added to his edginess. The thrumming carnival music and laughter from kids made him think of things he didn't have, things he hadn't even thought about wanting.

Damn.

He definitely needed to get laid.

Wearing reflective sunglasses worked in Adam's favor. He could scope out prospective company for later without anyone knowing, dodge left or right to avoid engaging women who always crowded his space, and he could ignore particular ladies—like Cindy, who'd just turned twenty—who he knew would only be trouble.

Just as turning thirty shocked him, so too did the idea of a female being too damn young. But there it was, the bald truth.

He was getting older and although he felt like a traitor to bachelors everywhere, he knew he needed more than giggling enthusiasm, a hot body, and blind agreement.

Pausing beneath the shade of a tall tree, Adam looked around at the colorful movement of summer T-shirts. So many women, yet thanks to this new weird awareness he had of his internal clock ticking away, he didn't feel a single prickle of interest.

He could blame his cousin for that. She was the one who'd started the nagging about him being a bachelor.

And once Amber had started, the others had chimed in and—

"Yer daddy wasn't a glassmaker."

Surprised, Adam looked behind him and saw Isabella Presley, the petite middle school librarian, seated on a quilt. She had her dark red hair in a high ponytail, her arms braced behind her and her legs stretched out with her sedate summer dress tucked in around her slim thighs. She'd taken off her shoes and for some insane reason, Adam zeroed in on her small naked feet.

She had painted her toenails fire engine red. Her feet looked soft, finely arched—

"Now see," she said in her southern-Kentucky accent, "that was a hint that I'd like you to move. Your daddy not being a glassmaker means I can't see through you."

Isabella hadn't been born in Buckhorn, Kentucky. No, she'd moved "up north" five years ago, yet retained her heavier drawl and an appealing accent. When she said "can't," it sounded like "cain't" and always made him smile.

"I got it." Pulling off his sunglasses, Adam moved to the side of her. "Mind if I join you?"

For an answer, she scooted over. Gazing out at the carnival crowd now that he didn't block her view, she said, "Take a load off."

"Thanks." Copying her, Adam removed his sneakers and lowered himself beside her. Their arms brushed. The slightest of breezes brought the sweet fragrance of her sun-warmed skin to his nose. Every part of his body noticed.

Trying to ignore the sudden awareness zinging

through his blood, he asked casually, "You supervising, too?"

"Nope. Just enjoyin'." When the breeze picked up, parting the leaves of the overhead branches and letting in the blistering sunshine, Isabella wrinkled her nose and squinted her blue eyes. "Sure is hot today."

Adam peeled his damp T-shirt away from his chest and nodded agreement. Heat and humidity left his khaki shorts limp. More than his shirt was sticking. "Low nineties."

"Swelterin'."

"Typical for this time of year."

"Mm-hmm." Suddenly she grinned.

"What?"

Lifting one lightly freckled shoulder, she said, "Just struck me funny, that's all."

Not following, he looked at her face, and smiled at the amusement there. "What did?"

"*Me* shootin' the breeze with *you*." She leaned a little closer until her shoulder deliberately bumped his again. "Buckhorn's most wanted bachelor, pausin' from his prowl to visit with little ole me. Ya gotta admit, it's amusin'."

With her tilted toward him that way, her face turned up to his, Adam suddenly thought about kissing. Hot, tongue-twining, consuming kissing.

With her.

Damn.

Since he'd known Isabella, he'd never once thought about getting his mouth on her.

At least, not seriously.

From the day she'd moved to his town, they'd been friendly, sometimes working together on school fundraisers or serving together on committees. Sure, he always enjoyed her company, but the fact that they saw each other within their careers at the school made anything more than friendship dicey.

Or at least that's how he usually figured it.

Now…not so much. "Issy," he teased back. "You flirting with me?"

Instead of denying it, as he expected, she lowered her lashes and gave a lazy shrug. "Honin' my skills for later, ya know?"

What the hell did that mean? "No," he said, trying to wade carefully. "I don't know."

"You're a big fibber, Adam Sommerville. You know in a few hours when the sun sets and the stars come out, you'll be findin' yourself some company. The glasses didn't fool me. You were scopin' out the prospects."

Had he really been so obvious? Rather than deny it, he asked the obvious question. "What does that have to do with you?"

Wearing the slightest of devilish smiles, she stared out at the crowds. "I'll probably be doin' the same, that's all. I figure by ten at the latest, the guys left will be the available ones who'd be interested. So I might try my hand at the pick-up game."

The pick-up game.

Why the hell did that annoy him so much? He wasn't her keeper, he had no claim on her, and…to heck with it.

Adam yanked off the sunglasses and frowned at her. "If that's your plan, why are you flirting with me?"

Indolent, and somehow sexier because of it, she sighed. "You weren't listenin'? Already told you I was honing my skills." She wrinkled her small nose. "Bein' a librarian means I know a lil bit about a lot, but pickin' up company isn't in my repertoire. Knowin' you aren't interested makes you safe for..." She looked up at him and smiled. "Practice."

Of all the... Feeling strangely annoyed, Adam stretched out to his back and folded an arm over his eyes. "You're nuts, Issy."

"Celibacy can do that to a woman."

From his eyebrows to his toes, Adam stilled. Plunged into curiosity, he lifted his arm away and stared at her. "Celibacy?"

She gave a self-deprecating grin. "It's been a mighty long time, that's all I'm sayin'."

He searched her face, a face he knew well, and saw no signs of teasing. She meant what she said.

Isabella, librarian extraordinaire, planned to get laid. Tonight. With some bozo from the carnival.

How long had she been without?

Adam thought back over the time he'd known her. Isabella had dated a few times, but he couldn't recall her being in any serious relationship. She stayed super-involved in the school, hyper-serious about kids reading, and she put in plenty of free time assisting disadvantaged kids and those with learning disabilities.

She stayed active, with work, charity, kids.

Just not with men.

So many times he'd wondered why she wasn't married with a few kids of her own. Anyone who knew her also knew she'd be an amazing mother. Smart, dedicated, friendly, caring...and now that he allowed himself to dwell on it, he had to admit she was cute.

Or maybe more like smokin'—in a seriously sweet and approachable way. It was her accent and teasing wit that made "cute" come to mind. That, and her understated wardrobe…fit for a librarian.

He reminded himself that her proximity at work remained an issue. Only at the moment, sitting here with her in the hot sunshine, breathing in her scent, that didn't seem to matter much.

To be honest, he could admit the friend vibe had originated with her. From day one, she'd relegated him to "work pal" status, without ever really giving him a chance to decide if he wanted to go for more.

And now that he thought about it, that sort of burned his ass a little. He wasn't a masochist and wasn't into chasing disinterested women, not when there were enough of the other kind to keep him busy. So then why-

"You do seem to wander off inside your own head, don't ya?" To take the sting out of that criticism, Isabella half smiled.

But it stung all the same. "I was just thinking."

"No, Sugar, you were daydreamin'." She lazily fanned her face and throat. "There's a difference."

Sugar? Adam knew she often addressed the kids that way. And when looking for new funding for her much-loved library, everyone was her "Sugar." But him?

First time.

She could easily charm students, parents, and the school board alike. But before now, she'd never openly attempted to charm him.

Suddenly the idea of a casual hookup with some other woman didn't interest him. Nope.

Adam wanted to seduce Ms. Issy.

Once decided, he didn't question himself. Why bother? The thought of having her was far more exciting than anything else had been in months. He felt more alive, and the sweltering summer heat had nothing on his rising internal temp.

His gaze tracked over her face to her throat, now looking dewy. "You want my help?" The second he made the offer, his heart started thumping hard.

He ignored it. This had nothing to do with his heart.

She took him off guard by stretching out next to him on her side, her head propped on a fist as she studied him. "Interestin'," she mused. "How exactly would you assist?"

Damn, when Isabella decided to flirt, she excelled. He should have expected that because everything she did, she did with perfection. It wasn't what she said, but how she said it.

How she *looked* while saying it. Sort of interested and amused and a little turned on.

Crowds milled past them only a few feet away. He felt the curious stares, heard the whispers.

And flat-out didn't care.

Visually tracing the curvy line of her body, he took in the shape of her slim thighs, the rise of her hip and contrasting dip of her waist, up to her creamy bare shoulders exposed by the narrow straps of her sundress.

Freckles had never looked more enticing.

"You have on sunscreen?" Even here in the cool, lush grass with the elm leaves shading them, she could easily burn.

After a priceless look, Issy blinked, then dropped to her back laughing. Not a loud or harsh laugh, but not a ridiculous twitter either. She sounded husky and sincere.

Enjoying her, Adam loomed over her. "You expected something more intimate from me?"

Eyes twinkling, she whispered with a smile, "Silly me."

How had he missed the length and thickness of her dark brown lashes, or the faint sprinkling of freckles over the bridge of her nose, or how her mouth, always free of lipstick, looked so full and soft? "Maybe I should explain the path of my thoughts."

"The path that led to sunscreen? Oh, I can't wait to hear it."

The ever-stirring breeze carried a baby soft tendril of fiery hair across her face. Without giving it enough thought, Adam used one fingertip to brush it back, tucking it behind her small ear.

Isabella's gaze smoldered.

From such a simple touch? And if so, how would she be when he had her naked and touched her all over? He gave a low growl that she answered with fast blinking, as if coming out of a spell.

Breathless, she asked, "What was that?"

He knew what she meant, of course, but said only, "What?"

"That macho sound you made." No hesitation from Isabella.

As if unsure, he suggested, "Reaction?"

Excited by the prospect, she came up to her elbow again. "You *growled* at me."

"I growled at my unruly imagination."

Her eyebrow lifted. She glanced at his mouth then back to his eyes, and breathed, "Tell me."

Tell her that he'd visualized her naked, in bed—with him?

Not a great idea. Yet. Shoot, they'd only just started the whole flirting business.

Twirling one finger, Adam took the safer route. “Let’s rewind to my thoughts.”

She made a face. “You gonna ask me about my last dental appointment?”

Damn, but she confused him.

“You know, since staring down at me made you wonder about sunscreen?” She flapped a hand. “There’s no tellin’ what you’re thinkin’ now.”

He trailed a finger over her silky shoulder, across to her collarbone, then up to lift her stubborn chin so those pretty blue eyes focused on him. “I was thinking about this soft, pale skin of yours. How fair and delicate you are. That’s what made me worry about the sun.”

Dubious, she shifted her gaze to her own shoulder, rolled it, and said, “I don’t know about delicate, but I do burn easily. So yes to the sunscreen. And now…about that wicked imagination of yours?”

A shadow fell across them and Adam looked up to see his cousin, Amber, staring down at them. Hands on her hips, a frown on her face, she chastised him with nothing more than a look of extreme disappointment.

Knowing he was caught, Adam sat up, winced at the new tightness in his shorts, and dropped his elbows to his knees. “What’s up, Amber?”

“You’re causing a spectacle.”

Issy, too, sat up. “We are?”

“*He* is.”

“I’m with him.” She gave a slow smile. “And honestly, Amber, I sort of like the idea of bein’ a spectacle for once.”

CHAPTER TWO

ADAM PACED IN front of the grill where fresh corn on the cob filled the air with mouth-watering scents. People lined up twenty deep, waiting to buy an ear. His cousins Shohn and Garrett ran the grill, but in five minutes he'd take over for Shohn.

Where was Isabella?

He'd had to leave her alone with Amber, and God knew no good would come from that. He adored Amber, everyone did, but the girl did like to meddle. Big time. And she'd looked disapproving, so heaven only knew where her unwelcome meddling would lead this time.

Naturally he knew why she'd been disapproving. Amber had a favorite, very insulting narrative she used to describe his preference for variety.

"You skate through women like it's a sport."

How many times had she given him that complaint? Usually he laughed at her.

He didn't feel like laughing this time.

Would she encourage Isabella to find a different guy? One more settled? A man who'd be better relationship material?

If Issy even wanted that.

Picking up a leftover guy at a town carnival didn't sound like anything serious to him. But he'd never gotten the impression that Issy was the "fast and easy" type, either. Everything about her screamed "nice girl," the type you brought home to meet your mom.

Adam knew *his* mom would love her.

He shouldn't care about Issy's plans, but he'd already worked himself up about it and—

Shohn shoved an apron at him. "Your turn."

Drawn from his thoughts, Adam eyed the utilitarian apron and shoved it back at Shohn. "I'm ready."

Shohn looked him over, caught his arm, and dragged him a few feet away to say, "I heard you were making out with Isabella Presley right in front of God and sundry."

What the hell? "We weren't *making out*." He scoffed. "We were talking."

"Horizontal talking? With you stroking her face?"

Snatching the apron back, Adam tied it on just to give himself something to do other than look guilty. "Horizontal, yes." As Shohn's eyes widened, Adam clarified, "On a picnic quilt, resting in the shade. But I wasn't *stroking* her." He'd wanted to. All over. With hands and lips…

But he'd managed to refrain that much.

"We were talking, period." About getting laid.

Or maybe it was laying each other.

Issy had put him into such a blind tailspin, he couldn't even remember everything he'd said.

"All right, don't blow a gasket. I just wondered." Shohn smiled at an elderly couple who strolled past, then laughed at two grade school boys who flew by with blue cotton candy faces and excitement in their eyes. "If I hadn't heard about her shaking off the old-maid mantle, I might not have thought anything of it.

But word has it that Isabella is looking to take a turn on the wild side."

Adam stared at him, horrified, suspicious, and damn it, a little jealous. "What are you talking about?"

"Rumors, that's all." Shohn whacked him on the shoulder. "Don't give it another thought."

Like he'd be able to think about anything else now? "Where'd you hear these so-called rumors?"

"From Amber."

Well, that explained nothing. Everyone knew Amber had very odd ideas about things—and often saw what others didn't.

His thoughts churning, Adam watched Shohn walk away.

"Hey, a little help here?"

He turned to see Garrett overwhelmed with a hungry horde looking for corn. "Right, sorry." With the apron in place, he stepped in and for the next half hour they served over a hundred ears of corn. Finally, once the band started playing from the stage at the other end of the lot, the crowd headed in a new direction.

"Wow." After dousing his face in icy water from the cooler, Garrett used a hand towel to dry off. "Between the heat of the grill and that broiling sun, I'm feeling as roasted as the corn."

"Yeah." Distracted, Adam fished out a chunk of ice and used it on the back of his neck. It helped a little, but with his imagination again on Isabella, what she might be doing—and who she might plan on doing it with—he was still too hot.

"May I?"

At the sound of that twangy voice, he jerked around and there she was, smiling at him. The evening sun gilded her gorgeous hair, highlighting the red and showing the richness of it. Her eyes were so very blue, her pale skin flushed. Between her breasts, her dress was slightly damp.

Adam felt himself reacting and didn't understand it. *What was it about her?* Besides her hotness. And teasing. And sweet little body…

She turned to Garrett. "He does this often, sort of goes off in his own head. Has your family ever had him tested?"

Amusement thick in his tone, Garrett said, "I don't think so, but I can make the recommendation."

"Might be a good idea." She looked at Adam again, tilted her head, then held out a hand. "The ice?"

He got it together and fetched her a fresh chunk. Anxious to see what she'd do, he stepped to the edge of the booth and braced his hands on the top beside the butter and salt.

Right there, in front of everyone—which mostly was just him and Garrett—she tipped her head back and rolled that ice over her throat and upper chest.

Lord have mercy.

"It is so hot." Lifting her ponytail, she tipped her head forward and teased the ice down her nape. A droplet trailed along her slender throat, over her shoulder and onto her chest. "Oh, that's better. Nice."

Adam swallowed.

After an elbow to the ribs and a sly grin, Garrett said, "I think I'll take a break. Man the fort, okay?"

"Yeah. Sure. Whatever." He peeled off his apron and stepped out of the booth to close in on Issy. "What do you think you're doing?"

"Coolin' down."

While heating him up. "You look like you're making a porno."

Her eyes flared…with delight. "I do?" She flashed her glance around but now that Garrett had booked, no one was close. "I was…sexy? Seriously?"

How the hell could she not know that? "You're getting me hard."

She started to look down.

Adam put his fingers under her chin, keeping her gaze on his face. If she looked, there'd be no "getting" to it. He'd have a full-fledged boner. "What's more, I think you know it."

"I didn't, but thank you for tellin' me." She licked her lips. "I've been tryin' to watch other ladies, to see how they flirt. Your cousin gave me some pointers."

He dropped his hand, blinked, drew a breath—and had to ask. "Amber?"

"Yes. She knows somethin' about everythin', doesn't she?"

"Sure thinks she does." Scowling, Adam looked around but didn't see Amber anywhere. He zeroed back in on Issy. "It's not a great idea to take advice from her."

"Then from whom should I take it?" She stepped closer, tipping her head back to keep eye contact. "You?"

The breeze was long gone, but as the sun faded behind the hills the heat lost its edge, making the evening air feel more tolerable. Still hot, but not so smothering. Around them, the carnival lights flickered on.

Feeling like they were talking about things other than advice, Adam said, "I offered, remember?"

"I remember that you failed to specify exactly what you were offerin'."

Anything you want. But maybe he should stop being so eager. Maybe he'd do better to tease back a little. Going with that plan, he said, "You could start by practicing your flirting skills on me."

"Oh, I *love* that idea." Smiling, she slowly touched his chest, stroked with her fingertips, lowered her lashes, and asked, "How's that?"

Hell, he felt that light touch clear down to his shorts. After clearing his throat, he said, "Effective." *He sounded like a strangling frog.*

"So if I seek out other guys tonight..." She walked her fingers back up his chest to his shoulder. "...you think I'd be successful?"

"At *what?*"

"I'm lonely," she complained with a sexy pout, her fingers still on the move, now teasing the damp ends of hair over his nape. "I need company, no matter how temporary."

Suspicious, unaccountably irate, Adam clarified, "Company, meaning sex?"

She smiled in a very provocative way. "That'd depend on the guy and how things progressed."

Not happening. Adam claimed her hand with his, brought it down to his chest and flattened her palm over his heart. "How about you slow your roll on that?"

Ferris wheel lights glittered in her eyes.

Or maybe that was a pissed-off glitter. Hard to know.

"So tell me, Sugar, you plannin' to *slow your roll* tonight?"

"If I'm with you, sure." *What the hell was he saying?* "Instead of you running off to sleep with some nameless—" *and lucky* "—dude, how about we enjoy the carnival? You can keep flirting. I'll tell you what works." Which so far had been everything. "And in the meantime we could have some fun." Not the type of fun he'd really like to have, but at the moment, he enjoyed her company enough that he could make a concession.

"Hmm."

Watching her take her own sweet time thinking about his offer bugged Adam big time. It should've been an easy decision. By now, other women would have said-

"Okay."

He released a tense breath.

"On one condition."

His teeth locked and he cocked a brow in query.

Looking very stern and determined, she said, "End of the night, no matter how things go otherwise, I at least get a kiss."

Whoa. After the craziness of this current interaction with her, Adam refused to make assumptions. "From who?"

"Why, from *you*, silly."

He forgot they were in the open, that kids and their parents milled around them. Neighbors and teachers. The principal. Members of the school board.

His own meddling family.

All he could think about was getting his mouth on hers.

Catching her narrow waist in his hands, Adam slowly drew her in. "If it's to be guaranteed, why save it for the end of the night? We could just start right off with—"

"There you are." Amber swooped in with Noel Poet in tow. Far too enthusiastically, she pulled Issy away and locked her to her side. "I've been looking all over for you, Isabella. Noel has some men for you to meet."

What the hell? Adam narrowed his eyes on Noel.

Noel immediately held up his hands. "Not my doing."

"Don't be modest," Amber said, flipping her long dark braid. "Noel easily racked up three guys, all of them perfect."

Damn it, he'd been about to kiss her. The last thing he wanted was for Amber to whisk her off to some other guy.

With biting irritation, Adam asked, "Perfect for *what?*"

At almost the same time, Issy said, "Really? For me?"

"Uh..." Noel looked like he wanted to make a run for it—until Amber took his hand. Then the putz melted.

It seemed to Adam that Amber and Noel made a most unlikely pair. But whether they admitted or not, that's what they seemed to be—sort of.

As a firefighter, Noel worked with Amber's brother, Garrett, which was where Amber had met him. Since then they'd been dancing around each other, not really a declared couple, but at every big community function they ended up together.

Amber had long dark hair and blue eyes.

Noel was blond with brown eyes.

But the contrasts didn't end with their appearances. Where Noel seemed quietly contained and often far too serious, Amber was bold, incredibly outspoken and carefree.

Sure, she was pretty enough to reel in any guy, but he'd assumed Noel had enough backbone to keep from being drawn into her scheming.

When Amber only smiled, Adam grated, "What guys?"

Shaking his head, Noel said to Amber, "I think we're interrupting."

"Don't be silly."

Noel said evenly, "I am never silly."

Amber just smiled at him. "Isabella already asked for my recommendations, and I'm giving them." Her gaze raked over Adam. "And that's that."

Issy laughed. "Well, I don't suppose it'd hurt for me to take a little look, now would it?"

Of all the… Adam narrowed his eyes. "You can't be serious."

"I'll be right back," she promised, and patted his chest—like he was a damned wayward mutt.

Stunned, Adam stared down at her. He had no idea what to say, so he said nothing.

Issy waited, but with his extended silence her smile faltered, and finally she looked away. "Noel? Are you ready?"

Very ill at ease, Noel hitched his chin. "Sure."

"I'll join you in a minute," Amber told them.

Still disbelieving, Adam watched Issy walk away, her hand in the crook of Noel's elbow, until he couldn't see her anymore.

"So," Amber started.

"Forget it." Beyond peeved at her, Adam headed back into the booth. She'd already done enough. No way in hell would he listen to some half-baked lecture from her.

Of course she followed.

"She's all wrong for you, Adam."

He leveled a sharp look on her. "Contrary to what every wimp in the county tells you, you do not know everything."

It was never easy to put a dent in Amber's confidence. "I realize that. But I do know *you.* And I also know Isabella."

Folding his arms over his chest, his temper on the rise, Adam said, "So what? You think I'd break her heart or something?"

She gave a surprised laugh that she quickly muffled with a cough. "No, I wasn't concerned about that."

Adam waited her out, his scowl not budging.

After another cough, Amber got serious. "I hope you won't think I'm gossiping—"

"Shohn already told me what you said."

"I only told him so he could tell you in case I didn't get to you in time. Even before I'd reached you two, I knew you were playing with Issy. *Everyone* was talking about it."

"Define everyone."

"People who'd passed the two of you. Ms. Marburl was scandalized. Little Chuck started singing that you had a girlfriend. When I stopped at the corn booth, Shohn didn't know where you were but he said you were due to replace him at any minute. So I told him."

"Told him that Issy is a wild child?" He snorted. "That's nuts and you know it."

"Oh, Adam." With a pitying look, Amber patted his arm. "You've known her all this time and yet…you don't really know her at all."

CHAPTER THREE

ISABELLA HAD A hard time keeping her smile in place as she walked away from Adam. She didn't want to meet any other men, and she definitely didn't plan to get intimate with anyone—well, except maybe Adam.

If he was still willing.

"You okay?" Noel asked.

"Course I am."

"You know, if you want, I can make your excuses to the guys. Say you got busy or something."

She peeked at him. "Is my disinterest that noticeable?"

"Afraid so." He paused with her under the lights of the roller coaster. They both looked up at the screaming riders as the coaster cars zipped by. "Amber has a tendency to bulldoze her way through life."

"She is confident." Sometimes Isabella envied Amber for her headstrong certainty.

"That's an understatement." Noel turned his speculative gaze down to her. "Don't let her bully you into doing anything you don't want to do."

Compelled to defend her friend, Isabella said, "She's actually been very helpful."

"And she always means well," Noel added. "I'll even admit that most of the time she knows what she's doing. But I've gotten to know her."

"Do tell."

One corner of his mouth curled. In a husky, satisfied-man voice he said, "Let's just stick to talking about you tonight."

Deflated, Isabella sighed. "If we must."

"Amber doesn't know men nearly as well as she thinks she does."

Oh, now that was interesting. "You came to this conclusion…how?"

"Because she's always playing games. And as a man—"

He was definitely all man.

"—I can tell you, we don't appreciate it."

"And yet," Isabella pointed out, "she's so often successful."

"How about we give a little credit to the men, too, okay? Yes, she hooked up Shohn with Nadine, and Garrett with Zoey, and Gray with Lisa—"

"You're ruinin' your own case."

Noel shook his head. "Making the point that while Amber might've pointed them in the right direction, or given a helping hand, she didn't make them fall in love. Each of the guys was smart enough to do that all on his own."

She peeked up at him. "That's what you think I want? To fall in love?"

After a commiserating smile, Noel took her arm and got her walking again. "I think you're already in love. What you want is for Adam to love you in return."

That insight so surprised her, she faltered a step.

How was it Noel knew that when no one else did? For sure Adam didn't suspect. If he did, he probably wouldn't be chatting with her now. She'd done her best to hide it, but she'd known for some time that he was the one for her.

It was party his great rapport with kids and his awesome contributions to the community . Adam was a very admirable man.

But it was also the way he carried himself, with pride and dignity, the way he pitched in to help others, the easy way he smiled.

Those dark bedroom eyes… She shivered, and admitted to herself that his body was pretty darned fine too.

But it was mostly his character, she assured herself. Sure he was great to look at, but she wouldn't love a man for his looks alone.

Realizing she'd gone too quiet, too long, Isabella stammered, "I, um…Why would you say such a thing?"

Noel stopped, faced her. "I saw you with him, and I'm not a dummy, either. Amber can play all the games she wants, but in the end, Adam has to know the real you. What it is you want or need, what you care about." He squeezed her shoulder. "Who you are."

Not knowing what else to do, Isabella nodded.

"So for now, if you want to follow Amber, go ahead. Just don't play so long that Adam mistakes your sincerity for an amusing pasttime."

Wow. Who knew Noel was so attentive and discerning?

Well, obviously Amber did. "She said I couldn't be easy. That I had to make him work for it."

It surprised her when Noel flushed.

Now wait a minute… Suspicion lifted her brows. "Is that what you're doin' to Amber?" When he looked even guiltier, a grin made her cheeks ache. "You *are*! You're makin' her *work* for it, aren't you?"

Noel walked on.

Delighted, Isabella hustled to catch up to him. "That is so funny."

"No it's not," he said.

"But this is great. Amber, caught in a game of her own makin'." She clapped her hands. "Totally great."

Pivoting to face her, Noel opened his mouth, hesitated, and clamped it shut again. "Just think about what I said, okay?"

"Oh, I definitely will. And thank you." This time as they started off, Isabella hugged his arm and even put her head on his biceps. A nice, solid biceps, she noticed. "You're a good man, Noel Poet. Whatever you do to catch Amber, I hope you catch her right and tight."

Little by little, Noel smiled and relaxed. "That's the plan." They turned the corner and there were three men drinking beers, playing horseshoes, and laughing loudly. One wore a firefighter's T-shirt, one was an EMT, and the other was Tucker Turley, the sheriff. She knew him well since he'd done plenty of community outreach programs at the school library. Turley was the handsomest of the three, which was saying something since they were all pretty fine. But Isabella knew Amber's cousin Kady was already sweet on him, and besides, he'd never, not once, looked at her with interest, and vice versa.

The men hadn't yet noticed them, and suddenly Isabella wanted to run.

"Cold feet?" Noel asked.

She bit her lip and nodded. "Would it be terrible if I just ducked away before they saw me?"

"No. But I doubt that'd work because Amber will probably bring you right back around to them. You're already here so you might as well talk a minute, right? No harm in that."

Just then Turley said, "Noel, get on over here. We need a fourth to even the teams."

"I have a better idea." Noel gently nudged her forward. "Get Isabella to play." And with that, Noel-the-traitor abandoned her.

"She's on my team," Turley said fast, drawing her in with a long muscled arm.

The other two protested, but after quick introductions and a few jokes, they got to playing. To her surprise, she actually had fun. She'd always known she had a competitive streak, but she rarely had time to indulge it.

After she and Turley won the first game, she tried to excuse herself, but instead she got traded off to the EMT as a "lucky charm," and dang if she wasn't on the winning team again.

That meant the firefighter demanded she join him next, and after three games, three wins, and two beers, she finally got free to return to Adam.

Unfortunately, Lisa and Gray were now in the corn booth, and Adam was nowhere to be found.

He hadn't waited for her.

Maybe Noel was right and she'd blown her chance.

Well, damn.

STILL WATERS RUN DEEP. That's what Amber claimed.

Issy wasn't prim or proper, she just respected propriety and knew when to mask her real nature.

A nature, Amber claimed, that would enable Isabella to use him up and then dump him.

Amber wanted to introduce her to a bunch of guys that, given a chance, Adam wouldn't let anywhere near her.

Hell, she might have met every one of those guys last night.

She might have taken one of them to her bed.

A strange red haze filled Adam's gaze until he shook his head.

No. He couldn't believe that.

In the small fishing boat, he crossed the lake. The family had a variety of boats and he could have used the inboard, the ski boat, or the pontoon. But Issy had a modest house back in the cove and sometimes, especially during the hottest part of summer, the cove got shallow—meaning dangerous to props.

The fishing boat with the small trolling motor was much better suited for the mossy, narrow passage.

Yesterday, after stupidly listening to Amber, he hadn't waited for Issy.

She wanted to visit other guys? He let her.

But after a mostly sleepless night he'd faced the morning with regrets. So now, regardless of what Amber had told him, Adam intended to talk to Issy.

First on the agenda, finding out what she had or hadn't done.

While he considered numerous possibilities, sweat trickled down the back of his neck and the sun baked his bare shoulders and chest. Even behind his mirrored sunglasses, he had to squint against the morning sunshine reflecting off the placid surface of the calm lake.

This early on a Sunday, few boaters were out to disturb the tranquility. Overhead an eagle soared. Along the shore geese honked at him and a flat, lazy water turtle rested over the rocks. Some fish swam alongside the boat while others leaped, making a splash.

Even with the mosquitoes and heat and the occasional drunk boater, Adam loved spending time on the lake. He could still remember, before his mom and Jordan had married, when Jordan brought them all to visit for the first time. There'd been so many kids and laughing adults. But what had struck him the most was the amount of love. Even as a very young boy, he'd felt it, craved it, and thanks to Jordan marrying his mom and adopting both him and his sister, Lisa, he'd become a part of that amazing family.

Jordan was a good man, a man Adam enjoyed calling Dad. A man to be respected by all. The day Jordan met his mom was the day Adam's life had changed—all for the better. Not that his mom hadn't done all she could. His mom was, and always had been, pretty damned terrific.

But Jordan had opened up a world of new, easier possibilities, and much of that centered around the atmosphere of the lake.

Adam could never get on or near the lake without a sense of coming home…for the first time, and forever.

As he neared the cove, Adam heard talking. Annoyance replaced reminiscing.

Did Issy have company? There were no close neighbors, so unless she talked with fishermen…

Or maybe she'd kept an overnight guest.

The possibility locked his teeth so tightly his jaw ached. Watchful, he continued on, unsure what he might see there on her weathered dock. He followed the curving shoreline, passed the concealing trees and shrubs.

And his eyes went wide.

Holy hell.

Peeling off his sunglasses and leaning forward over the hot metal seat, Adam soaked up the sight of Issy in a tiny blue bikini…halfway up a large tree.

Slim thighs straddled a fat branch. As she stretched forward, the strapless top of her suit looked in imminent danger of exposing her. Even as Adam watched, her hair came undone from some messy topknot and tumbled down around her shoulders.

The boat knocked into her dock, shaking Adam from his daze. He killed the engine, grabbed for the handle of the ladder that led into the water, and quickly tied off the nose of the boat. "Issy?"

"Shhh!"

His gaze swept the area and he realized she must've used the picnic table to reach that first branch and from there she'd climbed. She had the long strap of a canvas tote slung over her neck and one shoulder.

The tree hung over the shore, partial roots exposed to the constantly shifting water line. Taking in the picture Issy made with her bared skin and awkward hold, Adam trod across the dock to the land, asking more quietly, "What are you doing?"

"Tryin' to get this poor kitty."

Adam got closer, peered up, but he didn't see a cat.

He saw Issy. Mostly naked. Her legs were shapelier than he'd known, her breasts fuller. And that sexy belly…

At the sound of a loud hiss, Adam sucked in a deep breath and forced his gaze away from her body.

Oh, yeah, there in front of her on the branch was an orange cat. Young. Scrawny. And… "Do I see blood on him?"

"I think so." She reached out her hand. "C'mere kitty, kitty, kitty."

The cat arched up and hissed again.

Now with more insistence, Adam said, "Back away from him, Issy. He's feral. If he attacks, you're coming out of the tree the hard way."

"You think he'd—" Before she could finish the cat raised a paw in warning and gave a low, nearly demonic snarl. "Right. Backin' up." She scooted toward the trunk of the tree and looked down. "Know what, Adam?"

He stared at her thighs and thought about things totally inappropriate to the moment. "What?"

"Gettin' up here was probably a whole lot easier than gettin' down."

In her nervousness, her accent sounded thicker.

Adam cleared his throat; it wasn't his accent getting thick. "You have a ladder, hon?"

"In the shed over there."

"Don't move." With alacrity, he went for the ladder and was back in seconds, propping it against the tree and holding it there.

Issy stared down at him again. "Why don't you go do somethin' else till I'm on solid ground?"

He grinned. "No. I'm going to hold the ladder steady for you."

"But—"

Voice deeper, he insisted, "It's not safe, Issy."

She looked back at the cat, down at the ground, and started grumbling under her breath. She removed the canvas tote and dropped it—which only unveiled more of her stunning body.

Using the lower branches to help her, she maneuvered around. When one naked foot came down and felt around for the first ladder rung, it was all Adam could do not to groan.

Issy had a very sweet behind on her. And that teeny tiny bikini didn't leave much to the imagination. He'd seen skimpy bikinis plenty of times, just never on her. Maybe that was it, the reason his libido surged into overdrive. Usually Isabella dressed modestly. Very ladylike. Pretty.

But she never showed so much skin.

Now that he knew what she hid, how would he ever keep his hands off her?

Each rung she descended brought that pert rump closer to him. Occasionally she used the branches to help.

"What if I hadn't come by?" he thought to ask.

"I'd have figured out somethin'."

With her sweet, lyrical accent, he'd always known she didn't sound like a stodgy librarian. Now he also knew her figure didn't match the stereotypical librarian, either. The woman was flat-out smoking hot. *"Somethin',"* he said, mimicking her, "like what?"

She paused, looked up at the tree, then at the lake. "I reckon I could've dropped into the water."

"Hell of a drop." When she got close enough, Adam reached for her waist and swung her down the rest of the way. She immediately turned to face him, her chin up so she could see his eyes.

His hands were still on her naked waist, and he felt the dewiness of her skin, smelled the warmth of her from the hot afternoon sun.

He drew her closer.

She came up to her tiptoes…

Temptation had never looked so good. "Probably not a good idea with a pissed off feral cat in a canvas tote."

Confused, a little hazy, she asked, "What's that?"

"Your idea, about dropping into the lake?"

Her eyes almost crossed. "*That's* what you were ponderin'?" Giving a frustrated groan, Issy dropped her forehead to his chest. "We're here doin' the whole eye thing—or at least I thought we were—and you're contemplatin' ways my plan wouldn't work."

"Not really." Mostly he'd been thinking about saving the cat and then moving on to more rewarding pursuits. Like getting Issy out of that itty-bitty swimsuit.

"You are the most impossible man."

"I'm not the one who was sitting naked in a tree."

She lightly punched his side, then braced her hand on him. Then stroked. "I'm not *nekkid*," she whispered.

God, he loved her accent.

She coasted her open hand to his back, then up his spine. Voice gone husky, she said, "And you're wearin' even less than me."

She was still close, and he copied her caress, teasing the line of her spine—and making his own voice hoarse. "My bottoms cover a whole lot more." And good thing, since her nearness had physically affected him.

Leaning back, she took in his chest and breathed a little faster. "You shouldn't be here."

"Why?" He tensed, and automatically tightened his hold on her. "You're expecting company?"

Quirking a slim brow, she laughed. "Seriously, Adam? Would I look like this for company?"

His attention went over her again, and he inhaled. Softly he said, "Works for me."

She pushed away. "I'm not wearin' make-up."

"I've seen you without make-up plenty of times."

"No you haven't. You've seen me wearin' just the right amount of make-up to look like I'm not wearin' it."

Okay, he didn't understand that. Not at all. Screwing up his face, he said, "Come again?"

"I wear *subtle* make-up. You know, enough to make me look prettier."

With complete sincerity, he said, "You're always pretty."

She rolled her eyes. "Since when?"

Adam stalled. This was one of those tricky female questions, and he hated tricky questions. "Since…always?"

"Uh huh." She crossed her arms, which only further plumped up her breasts. "That's why every time we get too close, you say somethin' inane?"

Giving her a truth, Adam said, "You throw me off my game."

"Your game?"

"With women."

"Oookay." She switched her weight from one foot to the other, as if settling in. "Let's hear it."

Still looking at her hips, he said, "It, what?"

"How I throw you off."

This he could answer, no problem. "You're different from other women." How he wanted her was different. How she affected him.

How she burned him up.

"I'm waitin'." She even tapped her bare foot to the ground. "Expound on that, why doncha?"

"Okay, sure." This part proved more difficult. "You're mature."

After a three-second blank stare, she lifted the back

of her wrist to her forehead and slumped against the tree. "My, my, my," she said, and with her accent it sounded like *mah, mah, mah*. "Such heated praise. I do believe I might swoon."

Adam took his time looking at her body in the blue bikini. It had little pink flowers on it and looked both feminine and somehow vintage. With his gaze on the gentle curve of her belly, then her upper thighs, he stepped closer and murmured, "Let me try again." He slid a hand to her waist, and inhaled deeply at the silky warmth of her skin. "You're a smart, independent, confident woman who also happens to be sexy as hell."

Her lips lifted in the slightest of smiles. "Much, much better." She put both hands to his shoulders.

Good.

But he needed to know, so as he skimmed his lips over her cheekbone, he asked, "How'd last night go for you?"

"You left me," she breathed, her eyes sinking shut. "So it was rather disappointin'."

Hope took hold. "No hookups?"

"After chattin' with you?" Her gaze locked with his and she chided, "You should know better."

Just what he'd wanted to hear. "You were gone so long—"

"Sheriff Turly roped me into a coupla of games of horseshoes. But I did come back lookin' for you."

"Then I'm sorry I left." More than ready to taste her, Adam leaned down.

Isabella came up.

And the cat dropped behind them with a very annoyed screech.

CHAPTER FOUR

HOW HAD SHE forgotten about the cat? That poor animal was the reason she'd been caught in a tree in her tiniest bathing suit. "I'm a terrible person," she murmured as she took the tote bag and slowly knelt to face the cat.

"No, you're not," Adam told her, and then, "Let me."

"You as good as your daddy?" Jordan Sommerville was known to whisper a cow to sleep, or talk a dog through labor. The man had an amazing ability with soothing animals.

"No one is." Adam came down to one knee beside her. "But I've helped Dad plenty of times, so maybe I can manage. It'd help if we had something to feed him."

Giving her unspoken agreement, Issy moved back.

Adam ignored the tote bag and began speaking softly to the cat.

"Be right back," she whispered, and took off in a jog for the house. She ran in the back door, down the hall and to her closet where she grabbed a gigantic T-shirt that she dropped over her head. She raced back to the kitchen, rummaged in her fridge and finally found some cheese. It'd have to do. She hurried back to Adam…but pulled up short when she saw him sitting cross-legged on the ground, the cat lifting up to Adam's outstretched hand to be petted.

Awww... Right then and there, her heart completely

melted. No man should look that mouthwateringly good and also be so caring for animals. That's what she called overkill in the appeal department.

In a barely-there whisper, she asked, "What should I do?"

"Come in here on my other side—slowly—and have the food ready."

As she literally tiptoed, she whispered, "All I had was cheese. I'm not much for lunchmeat or hot dogs or any of that nasty stuff."

"Cheese will work." As she eased down beside him, Adam added, "And hot dogs are not nasty."

The cat watched her warily, braced to run, so she didn't debate the point with him. "How'd you get him to trust you so quickly?"

Adam now had his hand repeatedly coasting down the length of the cat's back, all the way to the tip of his tail. "I repeated some of the things I've heard Dad say, in the way he usually says them. It's worked before on kids at the school, but I'd never tried it on a feral cat."

"You sure he's feral?"

"I think so. But also desperate. She's way too skinny—"

"She?"

Just then the cat high-stepped away from them, tail up as Adam stroked her. Isabella looked, made a face, and said, "I don't see anythin'."

Amusement curved his mouth. "That's the point."

"Oh."

"Anyway, she's got a few superficial injuries, and she needs to eat more. And I'm pretty sure she has fleas."

That sounded horrible, all of it, and Isabella's heart broke just a little. "Poor baby."

"I suggest we try to get her in a crate, then we can take her to Dad. He'll fix her up."

We? Did he mean now? Starting to worry, she asked, "And then what?"

He rolled a shoulder. "Then you have a cat."

She considered it, and liked the idea. "What does that entail, exactly?"

Adam gave her a quick, searching look. "You've never had a pet?"

"No."

His expression softened, almost as if he felt sorry for her.

That didn't offend her because she also thought it was pretty sad that she'd never had a pet to love.

"Hmm…let's see. She could get all her medical treatment right away with Dad. Then you'll need a cat box, for sure. Regular brushings to help her stay groomed. Food, fresh water, the occasional treats… Overall cats are pretty independent. And given this one has been raised outside, I doubt you'd be able to keep her in."

Issy nodded, but said, "You mentioned your dad?"

"He's a vet."

"Right, I know that." He was the most respected vet in three counties. "But don't we need an appointment?"

Moving slowly so he wouldn't spook the cat, Adam lifted a hip and retrieved his cell phone. Using only his thumb, he cleared a passcode, pulled up a number, and put through the call.

A second later, Jordan Sommerville answered.

Adam explained the situation, checked the time on his phone, and said to Issy, "We don't need an appointment."

"Oh." For some reason, she blushed. "Um…good."

He went back to listening, nodded, and asked her, "Lunch with my dad okay by you?"

Lunch. With his *father.*

When she hesitated, Jordan said something else into the phone. Adam half smiled. "Dad said he's buying."

What in the world? What did any of that mean? And why would his father want to have lunch with her?

Confused, she asked, "What about the cat?"

"Dad will keep her overnight. We can grab a bite after he treats her."

Clearly she'd been out-maneuvered, she just didn't know why. Willing to play along, she pasted on a smile. "That sounds lovely. Thank you."

Adam listened to his dad again, nodded a few more times, and finally ended the call by saying, "If by some chance I don't catch her, I'll call you back."

Catch her? After that odd exchange, Adam turned his head, lifted a brow, and smiled at Isabella.

She wondered if he meant the cat, or her.

ISSY DIDN'T HAVE a crate so the cat was in a cardboard box and she wasn't happy about it. Catching her had been easy. Issy had put more food in the box and in the cat went. When he'd closed the flaps, though, she'd flipped out and hadn't settled down since.

Now changed into white jean shorts and a pretty sky blue top, Issy drove them to town in her small compact car. She swallowed repeatedly, winced at the cat's mournful cries, and cringed when it attempted to attack the box.

Adam had secured the box with rope and held it on his lap. He didn't want to take any chances on having a furious, feral cat loose in the small enclosed space.

"Shh, shh," he said. "It's okay, girl. Dad's anxious to meet you, and I promise you'll like him."

Looking very unsure, Isabella spared him a quick glance. "You *are* talkin' to the cat, right?"

He looked her over, from her tensed shoulders to her smooth thighs and everywhere in between, then said only, "It applies to you both." For as long as he'd known her, Issy had exuded confidence and competence. Now, though, she looked out of her realm.

"Adam?"

"Hmm?"

Her slim throat worked as she swallowed. "How come your father wanted to have lunch?"

He fibbed and said, "You're saving a cat. Dad respects that, so he'd like to meet you." *And he's cagey and intuitive and he knows I'm interested.*

But no reason to share all that when she already seemed so unsure.

Was it because he hadn't given her enough time to put on make-up? Not that Issy needed it, anyway. In the short time they'd been in the yard, she'd gotten some sun and her cheeks, as well as the tip of her nose, were pink. She'd pulled her dark red hair into a loose knot on top of her head, but little silky curls drifted around her temples, her ears, and her nape. Long brown lashes shaded her bright blue eyes and her slim brows continually drew together, telling him whenever she fell into puzzling thought.

Adorable.

Sexy.

And he wanted her.

Still.

More.

"Talk to the cat," she ordered. "You make me nervous when you stare."

Instead of looking away, he asked, "What's on your agenda after lunch?"

"Reckon I'll go to a pet store to grab some supplies. When she comes home, I need to be prepared."

After clawing a hole in the side of the box, the cat pressed one eye to it and stared at Issy. Or more like glared.

She gulped and gripped the wheel tighter.

Adam couldn't help but laugh. "I promise she'll settle down. But like I said, she might never be an inside cat. Which just means you'll have to be extra diligent about keeping fresh water and food available outside, watching for ticks and fleas, and keeping her treated."

They pulled into the lot of his dad's clinic. Despite being a Sunday, several cars were there. One Sunday a month the clinic spayed and neutered strays—this must be the day.

Issy parked, then hustled around to his side of the car. All the way in, she fussed and fluttered around as if wanting to help but unsure what to do.

"Take a breath," Adam told her. "It's going to be fine."

But like listening to a baby cry, hearing the cat's forlorn meowing kept her frantic.

A half-dozen neighbors sat in the waiting room, some with dogs, some with cats. They all stared as Adam and Issy came in. Being it was such a small county, he had no doubt Buckhorn would soon be alive with gossip that the middle school librarian was with the gym teacher.

And truthfully, that suited him just fine.

After only a few minutes they were shown to a room,

but then waited another fifteen minutes before his dad could join them.

Issy heard him before they saw him and she went on alert. Watching her watch the door, Adam saw her eyes go a little wider, her lips part slightly…

Why did every little thing seem so sexy?

Jordan stepped in with a smile. "Adam, Isabella. Sorry you had to wait."

Issy jumped to her feet in a rush. "Dr. Sommerville, thank you. It's obvious you're busy and I appreciate you makin' the time to see us."

Without slowing down, his dad smiled at her, took her hands, and smiled some more. "My pleasure, I promise."

Issy's "deer in the headlights" stillness amused Adam. He said again, "Breathe, honey. It's going to be okay."

His dad released her and turned his knowing gaze on Adam.

Adam, well used to his dad's ways, didn't blink an eye. But Issy, hands locked together, frowned.

After a slow smile, Jordan's focus went to the cat. "The little lady isn't happy."

Seeing Issy's expression, Adam almost laughed. *The cat*, he mouthed to her, then grinned when she blushed.

Adam set the box on a metal table and stepped back to let his dad do his thing.

He did it really well.

"Easy now, sweetheart. It's all right." Jordan kept talking, nonsense mostly, soft words to sooth the cat.

As she listened, Issy's eyes went heavy—as if mesmerized. His dad often had that effect. He could talk to a buzzard and make it coo. Many times his effect had carried over to humans, especially female humans.

His mom sure hadn't been immune.

When Jordan opened the box, Issy backed up next to Adam, expecting the worst after all the cat's snarling complaints.

Instead, as his dad lifted her out and cradled her close, all you could hear were her purrs.

"That's amazin'," Issy breathed.

"Dad has his ways," Adam murmured.

"I'd heard, but I'd never seen." Still watching Jordan, she let out a breath. "You have a true gift, Dr. Sommerville."

"Call me Jordan," he murmured, and twenty minutes later, he had the cat happily settled in a roomy crate with soft bedding and dishes of food and water.

"Tomorrow I'll get the results of the blood tests," his dad told them. "Once she's better rested, we'll treat her for fleas and any other pests. Do you have a name for her that I can enter in the medical records?"

Issy, still watching the cat with a very soft expression, shook her head. "I'm sorry, but I hadn't even thought about it."

"You're keeping her?"

She nodded. "Yes."

Adam saw that she'd already won over his dad, but that decision definitely cinched the deal. Jordan Sommerville was a sucker for anyone who cared for his beloved animals.

Satisfied, Adam said, "We'll come up with something over lunch." He slipped his arm around her, a move his dad noted, just as Adam had intended. He'd get his dad on his side, and some of the townsfolk.

Knowing Amber was out to set Isabella up with other men, staking a claim—even a temporary one—seemed like a very good idea.

ISABELLA WANTED TO melt under the table.

The second they'd walked into the diner, Sawyer and Morgan Hudson, Adam's uncles, had waved them over to their four-seat table. A waitress was beckoned to bring a fifth chair and now they were all squeezed together.

How in the world had she gotten into this situation?

Three of the four patriarchs of Buckhorn were currently smiling at her, and she just plain didn't understand it.

While they waited for their food, the men all engaged her in conversation. She knew each of them, of course. You couldn't live in Buckhorn and not know them.

As the town doctor, Sawyer ran a private practice out of his home, something he'd been doing since the day he got his medical license. In his mid-sixties, silver tinged his black hair and smile lines emphasized his chocolate brown eyes. He was still a very handsome man with an athletic build that she knew he'd gotten from working on the family property whenever he didn't have patients to see.

Morgan, only a little younger than Sawyer, remained a beast of a man, broad in the shoulders and thick in the chest. He had the same silver-tipped black hair but with vivid blue eyes that seemed to see *everything*. He'd once been sheriff but was now the mayor, and very involved in community service.

Jordan, the youngest of the three in his late fifties, had a very different look. Sun-kissed brown hair and deep green eyes. The only thing he shared with the others was his height and athletic build.

The entire clan—all of Adam's family—were physical specimens, beyond nice, and respected by everyone.

Figured the man she wanted most would be related to the town's leading family. Sighing, she accepted that she'd gone into it with her eyes wide open, well aware of his relatives. When she thought of Adam, it just plain didn't matter what complications there might be.

"So you're adopting a cat?" Sawyer asked.

"More like the cat adopted me," she said. "But yes, I'm happy to keep her."

"We have a project going to help feral cats," Morgan told her. "Where there's one, there's usually more. So if you see them, let me know."

Going cautious, Issy asked, "What would you do?"

Sawyer laughed. "Not what you might be thinking. No one in my family would take part in destroying an animal."

Letting the tension out of her shoulders, Isabella smiled. "Good to know."

"We TNR," Morgan explained. "Trap, neuter, release."

Fascinated, she asked, "How exactly does that work?"

"We get them treated, spayed or neutered," Sawyer said, "then notch an ear so we can recognize them later in case they get trapped again. Some can be domesticated, but some prefer to stay wild."

Jordan added, "Cats are more capable than you'd think. As long as they aren't growing their colony, they survive."

Adam's thigh brushed hers as he shifted toward her. "You know Nadine, Shohn's wife?"

"Yes." She cleared her throat to take the squeak out of her voice. "She runs that adorable pet hotel."

"Well, she's helping a lot. Uncle Gabe built her a huge structure where quite a few cats can live until they're adopted. It gives them partial access to the yard, and plenty of ways to climb. Uncle Gabe started calling it Nadine's 'cat sanctuary' and the name stuck."

His uncle, Gabe Kasper, was the only one currently not on site. As the youngest of the brothers, Gabe had once cultivated quite the reputation as a wild hedonist. But now, as a man happily settled into the domestic life with a wife he adored and three grown daughters of his own, the rep was merely a tool for his family to tease him.

His daughters were all sinfully gorgeous like him, but feminine, with pale blond hair and big blue eyes and the same flirtatious nature as their dad. Since he was the town's best handyman, Isabella had once hired him to do some roof repairs, so she knew him a little better than the others.

Worried about the feral cats, she asked, "What if they never get adopted?"

"Then they'll live out the rest of their lives at Nadine's," Jordan told her. "Safe and cared for, but of course, it's not an ideal situation."

"Those poor babies." She hadn't even met the other cats, but already her heart broke for them.

"The key," Adam said, "is to get as many of them fixed as we can. That'll at least slow down the population."

"Is there any way I can help?"

All the men grinned at her, and even more odd than that was Adam's look of approval…or maybe even pride—though that didn't make any sense. But then he draped a possessive arm over her shoulders, and the rest shared a knowing look.

"All right," Isabella said, flattening her hands on the table and glaring at each man, especially Adam. "*What* is goin' on here?"

CHAPTER FIVE

WITH PROPITIOUS TIMING, the waitress brought their food, interrupting what looked to be a small explosion in Issy's attitude. Course, she hadn't missed the way his relatives kept sizing her up. Although favorably, it still had to be a little disconcerting.

Leaning in, Adam whispered near her ear, "Relax. They just like you. That's all."

"It's more than that," she muttered back. "I'm startin' to feel like a virgin sacrifice."

Morgan guffawed, making Issy go red and drawing the attention of other diners.

Sawyer elbowed him. "I'm sure you weren't supposed to hear that."

"Not like we're deaf," Morgan said, defending himself.

Jordan smiled at her. "We're aging, but haven't yet lost our faculties."

Issy picked up a giant loaded burger that matched almost exactly what the rest of them had ordered. After saying, "You're all outrageous, that's what you are," she took a big bite.

And damn if that didn't earn even more approval from the elders.

Morgan opened his mouth, and Adam rushed to say, "You're going to scare her off. You realize that, right?"

"Is that so?" Jordan asked, munching on a fry while scrutinizing Issy. "You quick to turn tail and run?"

"No." She took another bite, eyed them all while she chewed, and after a drink of her cola, she asked, "Mind tellin' me why I'm being sized up, though?"

This time there was no shushing Morgan. "The boy's been hanging with all the wrong kind of girls."

Smiling with false sweetness, Issy chided him. "I presume you mean women?"

"I'll call 'em what I like, and sometimes, with Adam's preferences, *girl* is more apt."

"Mostly vacationers," Jordan said with a lot of meaning.

Issy cocked a brow. "What's wrong with vacationers?"

"They're temporary."

"Ah." She looked more confused than ever.

"You're different," Sawyer tossed out.

"I'm definitely local, if that's what you mean."

"Sure, that—and more."

Adam watched her so closely, he caught the glare she flashed his way. "You mean I'm *mature*."

So she was still smarting over that? Adam hid a grin. It hadn't been one of his finer moments, but damn, Issy threw him off—in wonderful ways.

"We mean," Morgan said, apparently speaking for all of them, "you've got more going for you than just good looks."

A blush crawled up her neck all the way to her forehead.

Jordan slowly smiled. "You know you're attractive, right?" Then to Adam, "You've told her she's attractive?"

That, and more, but he only said, "Yup."

Issy appeared momentarily nonplussed, then she let out a breath and pasted on a smile. "Thank you?"

The men all glared at him. "You're *sure* you've told her?" Morgan demanded.

Giving up, Adam shrugged. "Let's just say I've been less than smooth in my compliments."

That made his dad's smile widen, and the three of them shared more elbow nudges.

"Now what?" Issy demanded. "What's with all the..." She jabbed her elbows left and right, mimicking them and making them all laugh.

It was Sawyer who spoke up this time. "It takes a certain woman to throw a man off his game. We know the truth of that from experience."

Adam cocked a brow. "You're talking about when you met Honey?"

"And when Morgan met Misty," Sawyer confirmed.

"And when I met your mother," Jordan added. "When you were only four years old and hiding behind her knee."

Adam scowled. "Now wait a minute..."

His protest caused another round of guffaws.

"Oh, please tell me," Issy said, shooting him a teasing smile. "I'd love to hear about Adam as a boy."

That opened the floodgates, and the jibes poured free.

Oddly enough, now that Adam was out of sorts, Issy smiled and tucked into her food with renewed hunger, eating while they regaled her with goofy stories of him as an awkward kid.

But they spoke with unmistakable fondness, and every so often Issy sighed and smiled at him. Huh. So his uncles and dad were pretty good at this sort of thing. He should have realized that sooner.

When they finally wound down, the food was nearly gone.

"You must have a fast metabolism." Sawyer nodded at her nearly empty plate. "You don't look big enough to have eaten all that."

"I guess." She munched down a remaining fry. "I don't do well with idle time, which is why I was gonna spend my off day pullin' weeds down by the shore before I spotted that poor cat in the tree."

"You pull weeds in your bikini?" If so, Adam thought, then it was a wonder all the fishermen didn't congregate in that particular cove.

"Maybe," she drawled in that fetching accent of hers, "you failed to notice the heat. It's downright steamy."

"I'm sure he noticed," Jordan murmured.

"He's slow," Morgan said, "but not stupid."

With a growl, Adam said, "Maybe you guys should quit helping me now."

"Is that what they're doin'?" Issy pointed a fry at them and laughed. "Y'all don't make it easy to tell. But I can assure you, Adam needs no help."

That pleased the elders, but Adam wondered what the hell it meant.

Morgan cocked a brow. "He doesn't, huh?"

"Nope."

Sawyer looked at Jordan, who only shrugged.

Adam waited for her to expound on that, and instead she finished off the last pickle and two fries on her plate.

Amused, Morgan asked, "Dessert?"

"Not for me, thank you." She looked inquiringly at the others.

His dad declined. "I need to get back to the clinic."

"And I'll have patients showing up soon," Sawyer said.

"Then I suppose I should get back to pullin' my weeds." She wrinkled her nose. "It's the truth I've let things get overgrown. My schedule just stays so busy."

"Dating?" Sawyer asked.

Issy laughed and laughed, as if that was the funniest thing ever.

Adam didn't see the humor. She could have a date every night if she wanted. If Amber had her way, it might happen still.

To keep his dad and uncles from getting the wrong impression, Adam explained, "She's the school librarian, I think you all know that. But she also volunteers extra hours at the school. Isabella is great with kids, especially the kids who struggle with learning disabilities. She goes out of her way to ensure they all can read."

Finally done with her chuckles, Issy said, "Sometimes it's just a matter of findin' the right book for the right child. They're not all on the same level, and for a certainty, they don't have the same interests."

The men all agreed, alternately praising her and asking questions.

It struck Adam that he had a lot of reasons to be proud of Issy. Not just her beautiful face or understated sexiness, or even her sweet nature. She had…substance.

Real substance.

The kind you didn't mind showing off to your family.

And if he told her that, she'd no doubt mock him again.

He'd known other admirable women, he reminded

himself. A lawyer, social worker, a CEO. Smart women. Beautiful women.

But somehow, none of them had been the whole package; smart, educated, but still very approachable. Caring about kids and animals alike. Bold one minute and reserved the next. Sexy without seeming to know it, and sweet even when giving him hell. She had a sharp wit and a generous heart.

"We've lost him," Sawyer murmured.

"Coming to grips," Jordan guessed.

"There y'all go again," Issy said, her accent getting more noticeable. "Sayin' things I don't understand."

"Tell you what," Morgan said. "Why don't you come by for dinner Sunday? It'll give you a chance to get to know us all better."

"We grill out," Jordan explained. "There'll be swimming, boating, horseshoes and badminton."

"Shohn and Nadine will be there," Sawyer added. "Garrett and Zoey. Amber, too."

Morgan nodded. "Misty and Honey are leaving it as an open invitation, so more of the young folk will probably show up."

Adam felt his dad watching him, maybe waiting for him to protest, to make excuses. But hell, he wanted Amber to see Issy with him, to know she could quit with her match-making efforts. At least for now.

At least until…when?

Adam didn't know, and there was no reason he had to decide this minute. "What do you say, Issy?"

Big blue eyes stared at him with surprise. "Well, I…"

"You'll have the kitty back by then, and could bring her along. I'll give her a follow-up," Jordan offered. "Let you know how she's settling in."

And just that easily, Issy nodded. "All right. Thank you."

Something eased in Adam's chest. He needed more time with her. More than lunch, more than dinner with his enormous, pushy, intrusive family around. *Private* time.

He glanced at the clock on the diner wall. Still plenty of time for him to make a move.

With any luck, he wouldn't botch it this time.

ISABELLA STOOD IN her driveway, uncertain what to do now. After a quick trip to the pet store for supplies, they'd ridden home in an odd silence with Adam watching her intently, smiling every so often.

Maybe planning, though she wasn't sure about that part. They'd each exited the car in the same quiet way… and now what?

She felt out of her depth, and very uncertain on what should happen next. "I guess you need to get on home?" She winced after she said it, hearing the question, and the hope.

"Is that a hint for me to leave?"

"No!"

His gaze heated and somehow sensual, Adam closed in on her. "I'm not in a rush." He cupped her shoulders and drew her against him. "What about you?"

Heaven help her, the man could scatter her thoughts with a touch.

Feeling lame and hesitant—and a little like warmed gelatin—she gestured with a limp hand toward the back of her house and the waiting shoreline. "Well, after I put away the cat's stuff, I was gonna get to those weeds…"

"Planning to put your suit back on?" His chocolate

brown eyes stared down at her, making it difficult for her to breathe.

Pleased that he'd liked her suit—and her in it—she lifted one shoulder. "Maybe." *Definitely*, if it enticed him into staying.

He grinned, and it made him so handsome she wanted to go on tiptoe and kiss him silly. In fact…

Heartbeat racing, breathless, she inched up.

"Mind if I stay and help?"

Her gaze went from his mouth to his sexy bedroom eyes. "Help?"

"With your landscaping cleanup."

In a million years, she would never understand him. "You wanna stay and help me pull weeds?"

"Sure."

She shoved back from him. "Are we *ever* thinkin' the same things?"

He laughed. Actually *laughed*.

Oh, that got her irked. "My confusion is funny?" she asked in a deadly whisper.

"The idea that you'd not know what I'm thinking is." He moved close again. "Because I was thinking about how you look in that bathing suit…and how you'd look out of it."

Heat washed over her and it had nothing to do with the broiling sun. "You were?"

He gave a slow nod. "About kissing you. Touching you all over."

So maybe they had been thinking along the same lines.

He tipped up her chin and brushed his mouth over hers.

Holy cow, that was intense. A real toe-curler.

His warm breath feathered her lips when he murmured, "I keep reminding myself that I shouldn't rush things."

Blast. "Why not?"

The corner of his mouth lifted, and his hand slid along her jaw and up to cradle her skull. "Because you still have it in your head that you might want to woo other men."

Her brain was back there on that part about him getting her out of her swimsuit. She shook her head. "What?"

He kissed her again, firmer this time, his mouth moving easily over hers—and seriously, that did *not* help her to get it together.

He smiled down at her. "You've forgotten that you were going to practice your wiles on me?"

It sounded a little familiar…

"Have to admit, Issy," he whispered. "I'm looking forward to it."

Her house was private. They were all alone on the end of the lane, surrounded by a cow pasture on one side, thick woods on the other. *Go for it*, Isabella decided.

After licking her tingling lips, she went on tiptoe and looped her arms around his neck. "So how's this for wooin'?" Her breasts brushed his chest and her thighs touched his.

"Pretty damned good." He stared at her mouth. "Any guy who walks away at this point isn't into women."

"And this?" She brushed her nose along his warm throat, inhaling the potent scent of his skin, teasing him and teasing herself. Sensation curled through her as she kissed the warm flesh of his neck, a light touch at first, then with her lips parted, damper, hotter. She tasted him with her tongue, lightly bit him with her teeth.

His hands clenched on her hips, bringing her body into fuller contact with his so that she felt him, all of him.

Her pulse leapt. She wanted him *so much.* Not just for tonight. Not only for a weekend.

But *forever.*

Have to start somewhere, she told herself. Sex, right now, would sure get things started!

Licking her way up to his ear, she nipped his earlobe, brushed her lips over his jaw, touched the corner of his mouth, and…found herself being ravenously kissed.

Nice.

As her feet left the ground, she held on to him, loving the hungry way he took her mouth, the plunging of his tongue, his hot breath, how he groaned low in his throat.

Taking her by surprise and leaving her cold, he suddenly set her back on her feet, and their bodies no longer touched.

Dazed, she blinked and said, "Wha..?"

Adam stared along the drive, cursed, and grabbed her hand. "Come on."

Still disoriented, she couldn't get her feet working. "What…where..?"

"You have a visitor, honey. And we both need a minute before greeting them."

CHAPTER SIX

ADAM HAD A hell of a time getting his heartbeat to slow back to a semi-normal pace. He was hard, almost shaking with lust, and it didn't make any sense.

Issy had only kissed him. He'd been kissed before.

And sure, her scent intoxicated him. But most women smelled good. And were soft. And sweet.

How was she so different?

How did she affect him so strongly?

At the side of the house, his knees locked, his breath strained, he stared down at her.

She stared back. "Are you okay?"

A deep breath didn't really help, but it at least gave him a second more to think. A car door slammed and the sound of conversation—*a male voice*—carried from the driveway to where they stood.

Possessive urges swamped him, narrowing his vision until all he could see was Issy. Urgency kicked his heart back into a racing beat. He hadn't yet had her. He damn straight didn't want some yokel stepping ahead of the line.

"Adam?" she whispered, her expression growing wary.

He cupped one hand to her jaw, ran his thumb over her swollen bottom lip. "Did you invite someone over?"

Leaning her cheek into his palm, eyes closed, she whispered, "No."

The relief stayed just out of reach. "Then who—"

They both heard Amber's laugh.

Damn it. Umbrage stiffened his spine. *His busy-body cousin had brought a man to Issy's house!* What was she, a pimp?

Issy patted his chest, turned to kiss his palm, then whispered, "Just a second, okay?" She crept to the side of the house to peek around, taking care not to be seen.

Expression incredulous, her brows pinched, she ducked back and whispered to Adam, "It's the EMT I met at the carnival."

No, he decided. Not happening.

Yet as Issy pondered the situation, his indignation swelled.

She looked up at him. "You could sneak back to your boat and—"

"I'm not going anywhere."

That had Isabella tipping her head in a curious way. "If your cousin sees you here, how will you explain?"

I'm first in line. But no, of course he couldn't say that. It sounded horrible. She wasn't a prize to be won. She was a beautiful, intelligent woman who just happened to make him insanely crazed with lust.

And seriously, he didn't want there to be a line. Thinking about any other guys sidling up to her for any intimate reason—even a kiss—left him infuriated.

Only he didn't have the right to be infuriated. At the moment, he didn't have any rights at all.

Probably time to change that.

If he could.

"Yoohoo, Adam," she teased softly, waving a hand in front of his face. "You still in there?"

"I'll tell her about the cat."

One brow going up, Issy said softly, "Okay. So then why are you still here?"

Because I need you.

"She'll ask, Adam. You know that."

Before he could answer, he needed to know. "What are you going to do?"

"Get rid of him as quickly, but nicely, as I can."

There'd been no hesitation, and he believed her. He was a lucky guy.

Amber's voice reached them as she called out, "Isabella?"

"She's comin' this way," Issy said urgently. "Make up your mind."

Adam grabbed her in for a quick, firm kiss. He wanted her to remember he was waiting. "I'll stay out of sight. Soon as they're gone, you and I need to talk."

"We do," she agreed, coming in for yet another fast peck. "And I'll go first." Then she slipped around the house, catching Amber just before she would have busted them.

"Hey, Amber," Issy said in her soft drawl. "Sorry, I was down by the lake."

Adam stayed put, content to listen in.

"Just you?" Amber asked.

Adam recognized the tone. Amber already knew he was with Issy. How she knew was anyone's guess. But for sure, she knew.

"Uh-huh. So what's up?"

Glee sounded in Amber's tone when she said, her voice all silky, "You remember Wayne?"

"Of course. How are you, Wayne?"

For the next five minutes, Adam ground his teeth while listening to the byplay between Wayne and Issy.

Wayne wanted her. That much was clear. The way he spoke, how he laughed… Adam recognized the signs. Repeatedly Issy came up with excuses for why she couldn't get together, and repeatedly, Wayne found a new way to ask.

Coming on all hot and heavy, Wayne told her that he'd always been interested but she gave off "don't touch" vibes.

Ha! Adam glanced around at the guy with smug victory. Isabella had all but insisted that *he* touch her. That had to mean a lot.

"I'm sorry," Issy said for the tenth time, "but I—"

"C'mon," Wayne interrupted smoothly. "At least give me a chance."

Adam was about to intervene when from behind him, Amber whispered, "You big fraud."

He jumped a foot.

Damn it, he'd been so fixated on Issy's conversation with Wayne, he hadn't realized that Amber was no longer on the scene, and he hadn't even heard her approach behind him.

He jerked around to face her and caught her enormous grin. Pointing toward the back patio, he gave a silent order and with a shrug, Amber sashayed that way.

"So what are you doing?" Amber whispered.

"None of your business."

"Ooh, so it's that type of visit." She patted his shoulder, sharing her pity. "And right in the middle of things, Wayne moves in."

"He didn't 'move in'," Adam corrected with annoyance. "You dragged him here."

"Now, Adam," she chastised. "The man is more than willing. Trust me, he did not have to be coerced."

If he didn't stop grinding his teeth, he'd turn them to powder. "I thought you liked me."

She laughed quietly and gave him a hug. "I *love* you, silly. But I didn't know you were that interested." Holding him back, she asked, "You're saying you are?"

Adam opened his mouth—then snapped it shut. He wouldn't make confessions to his cousin before he even made them to Issy. "I'm saying you need to stop the stud parade. She doesn't need your help."

"Stud parade," Amber mused. "I like that."

Yeah, Issy might like it, too—if he didn't nix it real quick. "You have to stop." But he knew she wouldn't. Amber was like a tsunami. Once she got started, all you could do was brace yourself.

"Aw, what's wrong? Tell Amber all about it."

He scowled. "Don't talk about yourself in third person. You aren't the queen."

She laughed a bit loudly, and slapped her hand over her mouth.

Adam took her shoulders. "Amber, seriously." He bent his knees to meet her gaze at eye level. "I need you to give me a little time with her."

She sobered quickly. "Do you care about her?"

He did, but how much? Because he wasn't ready to figure it out just yet, he said instead, "I'm working it out. *We're* working it out. But it makes it tough when you keep tossing single men her way."

"Afraid of the competition, huh?"

For what Issy wanted? Yes. He might already be

too involved, but as far as he knew, she wanted to sow wild oats.

If she only sowed them with him, that could work.

But with Amber offering up so many alternatives—

"I'll give you a week," Amber said decisively. "Let's say…the picnic next weekend? Dad told me that he invited her to join us and that you further coerced her. So she'll be there, right?"

Um… "Yes?" Why did it still feel like Amber plotted his failure? It shouldn't have scared him, but determination glittered in her eyes and it never failed to set him on edge.

"Terrific." She put her finger in his face and leveled a firm look on him. "One week, Adam."

"That's not much time…"

She rolled her eyes. "You've known her five years, for crying out loud. Seven days is more than enough time for you to decide if you're interested in friendship, a fling or more." Triumphant, pleased with her own plans, she smiled, hugged him tight, and walked away.

From a safe distance Adam followed and heard her say, "Sorry, Wayne, we need to get going."

Wayne sputtered. "But I was—"

"I know," Amber crooned, her voice laden with sympathy. "I think Isabella has made other plans, though, so there's no point in dragging this out. Come on. We'll talk about other prospects while I drive you home." Truck doors closed and the engine revved. Amber yelled, "I'll see you this weekend, Issy. Make the most of your week!"

As her truck disappeared, Adam stepped out. Having a timeframe laid out pushed his fevered urgency to the breaking point. He needed Issy. Today.

Right now.

She had her back to him, watching the dust settle after Amber's truck departed. Sensing her melancholy, he stepped close to her, waiting, hoping she'd turn to him, touch him again.

The heat of her small body lured him, and he cupped his hands over her shoulders. Her scent filled his head and, unable to resist, he drifted his nose along her nape. "Issy?"

Resting against him, she whispered, "That talk?"

"Yes?"

"Do you think we could put it off for…oh, I don't know." Her voice deepened. "Maybe an hour or so?"

He had one week and he didn't plan to waste a single second. Gently turning her to face him and tugging her into full body contact, he brushed his mouth over her soft lips. "We can do anything you want."

"Perfect."

Adam held his breath.

"Let's get to those weeds."

WAIST DEEP IN the water, her hair pinned atop her head with sweat trickling down her temples and across her shoulders, Isabella cleared away weeds growing along the rock retaining wall. With every heartbeat she was aware of Adam a few yards up the shoreline, shirtless, his fair hair haloed by the sunshine, his shoulders bronzed.

At first, after Amber and Wayne had left, Adam had seemed surprised that she didn't want to go straight to bed with him. She *did* want to, but that would be nuts. They needed to talk.

About so much.

She didn't understand herself, and it made her sigh—which drew Adam's attention.

He glanced her way, pausing to swipe a forearm over his brow. "Everything okay, Issy?" With his reflective sunglasses in place, she couldn't read his expression.

But she saw his small smile.

"Yes." Sort of.

She couldn't stop thinking about Wayne, about how bizarrely insistent he'd been. He was a good-looking man with a noble job where he helped others. Tall. Charming. Bold.

But he wasn't Adam, so none of that mattered.

"You need a break?" he asked. "I can finish up here."

Talk about noble…the man had thought they would have sex. She'd seen that in his gaze. But when she suggested work instead, he hadn't balked. And now he offered to let her off the hook while he finished alone.

Isabella shook her head and wondered why she kept dragging her feet.

It wouldn't get any easier.

In a lot less time, Adam had accomplished quite a bit more than she did, so they'd already finished pulling the weeds around the yard. Once they finished along the retaining wall, they'd be done.

She heard a splash and turned to where Adam was last. All that remained was his sunglasses on the rock wall. Water moved around her and a second later he broke the surface right in front of her.

Lake water slicked back his hair, emphasizing his dark sinner's eyes. His scent was more pronounced, deliciously so. Issy touched his damp chest hair. "Guess you needed the break?"

"I need a kiss more." He brought her against his incredible body, making her gasp as his now cooled skin met her heated body. "What do you say?"

Nodding, Issy looked at his mouth and whispered, "I say yes." Always, yes.

She *loved* kissing Adam.

As he slowly lowered his head, his smile faded. He skimmed his lips along her jaw, up to her ear. "Jesus, you smell good."

She clutched at his shoulders. "You do, too."

He kissed her sensitive throat, and one hand dipped under the water to stroke her back, down her waist, and over her hip.

He leaned back to see her as he palmed her backside in the wet bathing suit bottoms. His eyes turned darker, heavy-lidded. When he hoisted her against him, she naturally put her legs around his waist.

Wet fingertips trailed over her shoulder to her throat, then along the top edge of her bathing suit top. "You ever had sex in the lake, Issy?"

Heartbeat thundering, she shook her head.

"You'd love it," he promised huskily. "And this cove is private enough to make it possible."

Scandalized, titillated, she whispered, "You mean..?"

He smiled and lightly kissed her mouth. "Not this time."

What a tease! "Why not?" Now that he'd said it, she wanted it, damn it.

"Because our first time I want to see you. Every inch of you. And that's not possible with half your body hidden in the water."

"Oh." Okay, that sounded pretty good too, because if Adam could see all of her, she'd be able to see all of him. A win-win.

Those teasing fingers played with one strap of her bra-top, ramping up her anticipation until finally he slid it down her left shoulder, down, down, until he could carefully scoop her breast free.

They both groaned.

Adam didn't kiss her—he was too busy looking at her, at the way his rough fingers held her pale breast, how his big thumb teased over her already taut nipple, sending ripples of sharp pleasure straight to her womb.

In a voice gone rough, he said, "I need to taste you, Issy."

Her thighs tightened around him and she watched as his head lowered to her, as his tongue circled, teased, and then as his lips closed over her, sucking gently.

So good. So, so *deliciously* good.

Letting her head drop back, she arched her body, bringing their pelvises closer together. Good Lord, she felt the pull of his mouth in amazing places. He readjusted so that the hand holding her bottom could slip into her trunks over her bare flesh. His long fingers searched over her, making her squirm and gasp, before sliding over her slick sex. He didn't press his fingers into her; no, he just teased, over and over, until she felt frenzied and couldn't stop her hips from moving against him.

Lifting his head, he groaned, "I'm on the ragged edge here, Isabella. Tell me you want me."

Words were beyond her. She was already so far gone that it amazed her. She tried to draw a breath but it sounded like a high-pitched cry instead. The water swirled around them.

With wonder, Adam breathed, "Damn," then eased

a finger into her, testing her, feeling the slicker wetness of her excitement. "You're close, aren't you, baby?"

Unable to think, she locked one hand in his hair, braced the other on his shoulder. "Adam…*please*," she breathed.

As his gaze searched over hers, it filled with satisfaction. "Whatever you want, honey." Bending back to her breast, he drew her in again, this time not so gently. He worked a second finger into her, keeping them pressed deep as she rolled her hips, moving in the rhythm she needed, ready to break. Close. *So close.*

But before she quite reached that critical peak, the sound of an approaching boat motor caught their attention.

Apparently better able to think than she was, Adam dipped them both lower in the lake, letting the dock hide them.

Gasping every breath, *so* incredibly close, Isabella wanted to cry. Her broken breaths sounded with disappointment and her body throbbed with need.

She hid her face against Adam's neck and struggled to catch her breath.

Adam stroked her back. "I'm sorry, Issy. So damn sorry." He glanced over the dock and cursed. After a quick soft kiss to her mouth, he freed his hands from her and let her feet drop to the muddy bottom of the lake. "Stay here. I'll take care of it."

"Adam?" she whispered.

He paused.

Even though she'd been the one about to climax, he looked as turned on as her. Color slashed his cheekbones and his dark eyes burned.

Isabella swallowed. "You don't want to hide again?"

"No." He tucked a wisp of hair behind her ear. "Never again."

She hadn't expected that, but she nodded. "They already saw you?"

"I don't think so." His hand settled against her cheek. "But I'd just as soon everyone know that I'm here, with you." He kissed her softly. "And why."

Her heart tried to lodge in her throat. "Oh." She wanted to ask why, but said only, "Um…Okay."

Grinning, he said, "How about you keep that agreeable mood? I'll get rid of these guys and get right back to you and then we'll see what else you might agree to."

CHAPTER SEVEN

THE SLIGHT BREAK while Adam spoke to two fishermen gave Isabella a second to think.

She'd been grossly unfair, and she knew it. Without any real honesty between them, she'd roped Adam in, making him think he'd be no more than a sexual fling for her. He assumed they could indulge a brief hook-up and then each go about their respective business, interacting at the school in a platonic way as usual, existing in the same small county without a single note of hard feelings.

He had no clue that it would kill her to let him go. He didn't know that, with Amber's help, she'd targeted him specifically.

Noel Poet's words kept ringing in her head: *Don't play so long that Adam mistakes your sincerity for an amusing pasttime.*

Physically, she wanted him. No way would she deny him now. But he had to know how she felt.

He deserved the truth.

She loved him, had for a while now, and it was past time he knew it, too.

While Isabella removed the band in her hair and slowly dunked her head beneath the cool water, the two fishermen indulged in idle chitchat with Adam. He appeared to know them, and didn't seem to mind when they made a few assumptions about finding him at her dock.

In fact, he encouraged them to see the truth.

"So you're helping her with yard work?"

"It was as good an excuse as any to hang around," Adam said.

Hearing that, Isabella went still.

The men laughed, wished him luck in winning her over—*ha!*—and finally moseyed on.

But they were no sooner gone than another boat showed up, this time a pontoon with Turley and the fireman she'd met at the carnival. She didn't remember his name, but Adam helped remind her by saying, "Turly, Bear. How ya' doing?"

Bear, that's right. How could she have forgotten that?

"Where's Isabella?" Bear asked.

In a not-so-nice tone, Adam replied, "Why do you ask?"

Turly laughed. "A day late and a dollar short, Bear."

"Is that so?" Bear asked, presumably to Adam since that's who answered. "Did I miss my chance?"

"You never had a chance," Adam told him. "For damn sure, you won't get one now."

Clinging to a dock pier, Isabella blinked. She had no idea how to take that. Staking a claim? On *her*?

But…for how long?

With the brief moment of privacy, she'd gathered a modicum of control. There was no reason to leave Adam to deal with the men on his own, so, after a deep breath, she hoisted herself up to the side of the dock.

As she stood, she said, "Hi guys."

All three men faced her. A beat of tense silence made her squirm. She tried a smile to put them at ease.

Turly pushed back his sunglasses and whistled.

Bear stared as if he'd never in his life seen a woman in a swimsuit, then swallowed audibly.

For crying out loud. Hers was more modest than many, not that you could tell by his reaction. In fact, the way he stared, she was starting to feel naked when she knew most women on the lake were in skimpier bikinis.

She was trying to think of something to say when Adam appeared in front of her. "If there's nothing else, you guys can get lost."

Finally regaining his wits, Turly burst out laughing.

"Now wait a minute," Bear protested as the boat motor rumbled to life. "Amber said—"

"Amber was obviously wrong," Turly told him, and he took a sharp turn, angling the boat back out of the cove. Bear craned his neck to keep her in his sights, still trying to protest when they disappeared from view.

"That was so odd."

Adam turned to stare down at her. "You just gave Turly a mild heart attack." His hand opened on her waist, his thumb moving over her belly.

"I don't know—"

"You are sexy beyond belief."

Isabella would have denied that, but he kissed her. Not a tentative kiss, but a 'Let's pick up where we left off' hot, wet, involved-tongue kiss.

Clinging to him, she kissed him back, and all the same sensations swamped her, putting her right back on that precipice of release.

Adam inched away to look at her. "Your house?" he asked hopefully as he trailed his fingertips over her still damp shoulder.

Her house, where they could be alone, where boaters couldn't intrude.

Where she could finally have Adam Sommerville in all the ways she wanted. "Yes," she breathed.

No, wait. Not *all* the ways she wanted…because she wanted him forever.

He started to move but she stayed him. "Hold up." God, this was harder than she'd ever imagined. "I need to tell you somethin' first."

"All right." He didn't pressure her, just looped his arms around her waist, studied her face, and waited.

SEEING THE RETICENCE in Issy's expression, Adam frowned. Something wasn't right.

Only a few minutes ago, she'd been ready to come apart from his touch. He'd felt the wetness of her slicking his fingers, felt her heat and the way she clung to him, heard the incredibly sexy sounds she made as her release grew near.

She wanted him, he knew that. Hell, she hadn't been shy about letting him know. But now, when they were finally ready to end the torture, she kept him standing on the dock.

She looked worried, and he didn't like that. When they got together—*and please, let it be now*—he wanted her with him one-hundred percent.

Forcing himself to patience, he asked, "What is it, honey?"

A deep inhalation lifted her breasts. Beautiful, full breasts.

She braced herself—why, he didn't know—and scooted closer, kissing his chest, his shoulder. "I'm hopin' you don't get mad."

They were ready to have sex; why the hell would he be mad?

"And I hope you don't change your mind. I really, really hope that."

"Change my mind about wanting you? Not going to happen." He needed her. He was so hard he hurt, but now, with this build-up of something, his gut cramped a little. "Whatever it is—"

"I love you," she blurted.

Adam fell back a step and almost went off the side of the dock. Issy grabbed him, helping him regain his balance. He stepped them both forward, away from the edge.

Talking ninety miles a minute, Issy held on to him. "I've loved you for a long time! I'm so sorry I didn't say somethin' earlier. But I was afraid to. I didn't think... that is, I know you don't feel the same."

He opened his mouth—but nothing came out. He needed a second to think.

"*I love you*," she said again, her voice filled with longing. "But I want you, too."

Want, as in sexually? That was good...or was it?

"You're confused," she said, her eyes big and filled with dread. "Of course I understand why. Please, please know that I don't expect anything. I mean, I want things. I hope for things. But for this—" She gestured between them. "—that's a given, okay?"

Stupidly, he shook his head. "This?"

"Sex. Us. We can do that regardless. We *will* do that. I mean, I *want* to and hope I'm not scarin' you off. But if you don't anymore, I promise I won't fuss or anything." Utterly agonized, she wound down, then whispered desperately, "I love you."

She was so uncertain because she didn't know he felt. But then, *he* didn't know how he felt.

"I swear," she added, "I wouldn't tease and make you think… I wouldn't lead you on only to throw out this emotional baggage and then bail on you. Noel told me—"

He latched onto that. "Noel?"

She nodded fast, her hands still holding on to him as if she feared he might run screaming away from her.

Because she loved him.

"Noel told me not to play Amber's games. He said—"

More confusing by the moment. Adam put a finger to her mouth and shook his head. He needed a second. Or maybe a day.

He needed *her*.

"What does my busy-body cousin have to do with this?"

Issy shied away. "I, um…"

"Isabella?"

Hearing him use her full name, she lifted her chin. "I told her I loved you. That is, she offered to fix me up with some different guys and I told her it was *you* I wanted, that it was because of you I hadn't been datin' and…" She trailed off, becoming subdued once more. "Stuff."

"Stuff," he repeated stupidly. "What *stuff*?"

She shrugged. "Sex stuff."

Poleaxed, Adam struggled to catch up. So she'd been celibate… "Because you want me?"

She nodded, then inhaled again.

And this time it was Adam bracing.

"I want you so much, Adam." Her small hand moved over his chest, then up his shoulder to the back of his neck. Gaze pleading, she whispered, "Today. *Right now.* Okay? Please?"

He had no idea if he should be relieved or not. "I want you, too."

Her smile came, then went. "But…and this is the tricky part."

Oh good. A *tricky* part. He worked his jaw. "Let's hear it."

"If you're not…if you don't have feelins for me, too, then…" She winced. "It should probably just be this one time."

It took a second for that to sink in. "One time…" sounded completely inadequate.

Staring up at him, Issy nodded. "One time to relieve the itch, or satisfy your curiosity or whatever it is you're feelin' for me." Her gaze moved over him, hopeful, and damn but he saw the love.

For him.

"Amber told me you needed a nudge. She said you were so determined on bein' a bachelor that you might not even recognize your own feelings. So I went along with her game."

"Game?"

She bit her lips and nodded. "To give you that nudge."

"By flaunting other possible guys in front of me?"

She winced, guilt stealing her gaze away so that she stared at the lake. "See, that was the plan at first. But before I could even give it a go, you approached me at the carnival and I wasn't interested in that game anymore." Her gaze returned to his face. "Only Amber didn't know that, so she carried on. And between us, everything seemed to happen at once."

Because he'd already been changing—without

Amber's damned intrusion. *When he saw his cousin again—*

"If you feel more for me," Issy said quietly, drawing him back around, "then I'm here. I'm yours."

His heart leapt at that, then started hammering. *I'm yours.* Elation coursed through him, ramping up his possessiveness, further sharpening his need, though how that was possible he didn't know. He'd already wanted her more than any other woman, but now… what he felt wasn't even in the same stratosphere of anything familiar.

"If that's not what you want," she continued, her expression watchful, wary. "If you don't feel that way about me, then please, for my sake, let's make it only once."

The *once* being… "You mean this time? Here and now?"

She nodded. "*Just* this time, if all you want is sex."

Still feeling a little numb and far too slow, Adam asked, "Do I have time to think about it?"

She gave a nearly hysterical laugh, but quickly cut it off with a hand over her mouth. Encouraged that he was still here, talking about it, she nodded fast. "Yes, of course." She stroked her hand down his chest. "We could go up to my house now and…"

He cupped her face. "Sate our curiosity?"

"Yes. And you can think about it then, and later, and…take all the time you need."

Never in his life had he felt so lost in confusion. Or so turned on. It wasn't just the lust churning through his bloodstream, leaving him almost lightheaded.

His chest felt…full.

With emotion.

He wasn't yet sure if that emotion was fear, or relief, or…what the hell it might be. There was just too damned much of it. So much, he thought he might choke on it.

He needed to act, so he did. Stepping to the boat, he retrieved his wallet, jammed it into his pocket, and bounded back out to the dock where he scooped her up and damn near ran up the hill to her house.

"Your sunglasses!" she said. "They're still on the wall—"

Adam kissed her. He didn't care about his sunglasses. He didn't care about his cousin's warped games. He wouldn't have cared about his wallet…except that's where he kept an emergency condom, thank God.

He wanted Issy. He had her in his arms.

Curiosity, hell. His need was so powerful, it felt like a ticking time bomb.

CHAPTER EIGHT

LUCKILY THE BACKDOOR of her house wasn't locked up, because Adam didn't want to put her down. Practically jogging, he raced to the small patio, adjusted her so he could slide the door open, and found himself in her kitchen. His heart thundered. "Which way?"

Squeezing him, her face against his neck, Issy said breathlessly, "Down the hall, last room to the right."

He passed other rooms, but didn't care. As he rushed into her bedroom, he temporarily stalled.

It was…pretty. Girly, even. Braided rugs covered the hardwood floor. White and sky blue gauzy curtains coordinated with a patchwork quilt done in wildflower patterns.

Another facet to her personality.

Then he forgot about her room and lowered her to her feet.

"I'm wet," she said.

"Good to know." Reaching around her, he untied the bra top to her suit.

Issy held it in place. "No, I mean my hair and—"

He kissed her, *devoured* her, until she forgot about everything but him. Her arms came around his neck and he tossed the wet top aside, then slid his hands into her bottoms.

"Oh." When he went to his knees, taking the bottoms with him, Issy braced her hands on his shoulders.

Breathing hard, Adam sat back on his heels and gazed at her naked body. Long ropes of wet hair trailed around her pale breasts, leading his attention to the dip of her narrow waist and slight curve to her belly, then down the length of her slender thighs. Damn, she was perfect.

Perfect for him.

Pulling her to him, he put a gentle love bite to her ribs, then her belly…and her inner thigh.

He rubbed his nose over her skin, drinking in her scent, filling his head with the aroused, rich, sun-warmed female fragrance. "God," he groaned, turning the soft bites to open-mouthed kisses, tasting her, wanting to eat her up.

"Adam." Tenderly, she coasted her fingers through his hair. "Come up here to me."

Instead he tumbled her onto the bed, then settled over her. Long lashes half lowered in a heavy, aroused expression of excitement. "Stay just like this," he told her. "Promise me."

She nodded.

Levering up and off her, Adam dug in his back pocket, removed his wallet and opened it to find the lone condom tucked away.

"Aren't you resourceful," Issy teased.

"I don't take chances." Except that here, with her, he was. *I love you.* Her words kept playing in his head, over and over and each damn time it made his muscles tighter.

And his dick harder.

He needed to be inside her—but first he needed her

back to the breaking point, gasping, squeezing him, moving against him…

Jesus. Holding the condom packet in his teeth, Adam looked at her while shucking off his shorts.

Her lips parted and she rose to one elbow.

"Ah-ah," Adam told her after tearing open the foil packet. "You promised not to move." He rolled on the rubber and came down over her again. "I like you just like this."

Breathing harder, she nodded. "I like this too." One of her legs hooked over his and she coasted her foot up the back of his calf, then his thigh, until she could wrap her leg around him. "You feel so good."

He held both her breasts, bringing them together and bending to kiss her nipples, to lick at her, suck on her—make her urgent again.

She got there pretty quickly.

"Adam." Arching her back and better offering up her breasts, she held his head to her.

"I want you to come for me."

"Yes." She tried to move under him, probably hoping to hurry him along.

Wasn't going to happen.

Didn't matter that he went nuts with wanting her, he needed to know it was good for her—and that meant letting her go first.

"Take it easy."

"I've been wantin' you too long."

He started to say, *Me too*. But was that true? At the moment, it felt like he'd been waiting a lifetime for her. He said instead, "Shh…" and kissed his way down her body.

Issy squirmed, gasped, purred with each small nibble, leisurely lick, or soft suck.

Slipping off the side of the bed, he caught her hips, pulled her to the edge, and arranged her legs over his shoulders.

"Adam?"

The excited, rasping way she said his name turned him on even more. He nibbled his way from her inner knee to the top of her thigh, parted her gently with his fingers, and covered her with his mouth.

"Oh...*wow*." Her tender thighs closed reflexively against his jaws as Adam moved his tongue over her, in her, then up to her small, swollen clitoris.

As he drew on her, she cried out, her hips lifting. He splayed one hand over her belly to hold her still and lifted the other to her breast, teasing her nipple.

She tasted so good and smelled even better and Adam knew he could spend an hour eating her. But far too soon she quickened, her thighs tensing, her belly clenching, hands fisted in the quilt and—

She cried out, at first high, then low and raw as her body squirmed and the pleasure drained her.

The second she went lax, while she was still gasping, Adam rose over her, pressed one leg wider, and sank into her with a vibrating groan. He wouldn't last, knew it, hated it, but already a hot rush of release stole his resolve and his senses.

Limply, Issy hugged him, her lips moving over his shoulder as his hips pounded against her. He was almost gone when he felt her tightening around him again. He squeezed his eyes and clenched his teeth and concentrated, holding off his own release, holding, holding—

until she broke. Then he lifted up to see her, his gaze locked on hers, and finally he let himself go.

AT SOME POINT Adam had turned to his back and brought Isabella with him. She rested atop him, her cheek to his chest, her body utterly lax.

Every so often Adam petted her, or kissed her shoulder or temple, occasionally fondling her backside.

She sighed and knew nothing could ever be more perfect.

Unless he loved her.

After waiting a half hour, the silence started to get to her. She came up to her elbows and found Adam wide awake, watching her with dark eyes and a disturbing intensity.

"Hey," she said, suddenly feeling shy.

He tucked back her hair. "Hey, yourself."

"That was..." Seriously, she had no words.

"Yeah." Using both hands he cupped her face and brought her down for a gentle kiss. "Very much so."

So he'd felt it too? Nice.

Hopefully he'd want to do it again, but she just didn't know. "Did you think about...you know?" She toyed with his chest hair and dared a quick peek at him. "What I said."

With deep concentration, he traced her mouth with one fingertip. "Thought about it, thinking about it, will think about it a lot more, I'm sure."

What did that mean?

He continued to touch her, lifting one of her hands so he could kiss each fingertip.

Because she had no idea what they were doing, Isabella said, "Tomorrow I'll go get the cat."

"Mmm." He kissed her wrist. "Want me to go with you?"

Did that mean..? If he offered to spend more time with her…was that an agreement of sorts to give a relationship a chance? She studied his expression, but other than looking sated, and tender and somehow cocky, she couldn't tell what he thought or felt.

"So…"

He smiled. "So?"

Okay, now her temper was starting to prickle. "Not to pressure you, but..?"

When his brows pinched, she quickly retrenched and said, "Never mind. Surprise me."

He turned her beneath him, stared at her, then took her mouth in a long, deep kiss. By small degrees, he lifted away and smiled down at her. "How about I call you in the morning?"

After that kiss, and with the feel of his big, firm body over hers, it took her a second to get her thoughts together. "Sure. That'd be great." Playing it cool, she shrugged. "If that's what you want."

His gaze dropped to her mouth. "I want you."

She reminded him, "You've had me."

"I want you again."

Her breath caught. "You mean…now?"

"Yeah, but I only had the one rubber."

Damn. "I should've bought some."

That made him grin again. "How about I bring more with me tomorrow?"

Her throat went tight. Trying to be firm, to stick with what she knew would be best, Isabella said, "I'd like that."

"Good." He bent to nibble on her shoulder, and honestly, the way the man nibbled got her very heated, very quickly.

"Adam, remember, I told you—"

"I know." He gathered her close, his arms framing her head, his mouth pressing a kiss to her forehead, the bridge of her nose, and then her chin. "I'll always be honest with you, Issy."

Oh no. She wasn't sure she wanted his bald honesty. She swallowed, nodded, and said warily, "Okay."

"I want more with you. This one time, stupendous as it might have been, wasn't near enough. Tomorrow won't be enough, either. But I don't know what will be enough. A lot happened, and it happened fast."

She understood that. "You noticin' me, and acting on it, and—"

He shook his head. "I've always noticed you, you need to know that. But until yesterday you always seemed real untouchable. I'm not sure what was different, but when I saw you at the carnival, sitting on that quilt with your shoes off—"

She laughed. "So nekkid feet did it for ya, huh?"

"It wasn't just the 'nekkid' feet," he teased, mimicking her accent. "You flirted with me. You went from mere politeness to teasing and giving off a vibe—"

"I have a vibe?" She loved the sound of that.

"A very sexy vibe."

"Huh." This after-sex chitchat was pretty darned interesting. A woman could learn all sorts of things. "Amber coached me. She told me to—"

"Hush." Pressing a finger to her lips, Adam interrupted her. "I can't talk about my cousin while lying naked on you, thinking the things I'm thinking. The two just don't mix."

Excitement bubbled up. "What're you thinkin'?"

"Raunchy things," he whispered. "Sweet things. Nasty, hot, sexual and tantalizing things."

Her toes curled, and she asked, "About me?"

"Don't say it like that surprises you." He laughed and kissed her again, then sat up. "You're gorgeous, especially like this."

"Nekkid."

"Yeah."

She laughed, too. So much happiness cocooned her, she wanted to get up and dance.

But she'd definitely get dressed before she did anything like that.

Adam Sommerville, Buckhorn's most sought after bachelor, was in her bed. They'd made love—wonderful, hot, mind-blowing sex—and now she got to look at his wide, bare back while he sat on the side of her bed teasing her.

Feeling daring, she asked, "Do you need to leave?"

His gaze locked on hers. "Not unless you want me to."

Heck no. If she could have her way, he'd never budge. "Gettin' hungry?" she asked. "I could cook."

"I don't want you to go to any trouble. We could order pizza or something."

Isabella wrinkled her nose. "I like to cook."

"If you're sure, then yes, I'm starved." As if he'd been doing so for years, he idly cupped her breast. "How about we compromise and I'll grill? We can sit out back and enjoy the sunset."

Ohhh. So romantic. "I'd love that."

He stood and stretched.

And in the process he almost turned her into a puddle of excited hormones.

So far, this was all going so well.

Isabella couldn't wait to share with Amber. Not only did she count Amber as a friend and confidante, but she needed to let her know that things had definitely changed.

Before Amber introduced her to any other men, Isabella wanted to put all her concentration on making things work with Adam.

At the moment, that was about all she could handle.

CHAPTER NINE

SHE NAMED THE cat Cupid. Seemed appropriate to Adam, considering the cat had played a hand in helping him get closer to Issy. All week he watched her with Cupid, and it brought back memories of other things.

She bought the cat toys, and he thought of the times he'd seen her gift books to underprivileged students.

She groomed Cupid, and he thought of the time he'd walked into the library and found her fixing a girl's hair when one of her braids had come undone. When she'd finished, that braid looked better than the other, so she'd redone the second one also, neatly tying ribbons to the ends of both. The girl had given her a shy smile, a fast hug, then taken the book Issy offered and went off to read.

He could still recall how he'd stood there, watching Issy as she smiled after the child, a look of tenderness in her eyes. No one would ever call her *just* a librarian, because she was so much more. Librarian, fighter for the underdog, motivated giver, caring supervisor, and sexy manipulator... Isabella Presley was a complex, complicated, fascinating woman with an enormous capacity for love.

That day in the school library, she'd been wearing a below-the-knee black pencil skirt with flats and a tucked-in white blouse, her hair in a twist at the back of her neck. He'd teased himself with the thought of kissing her nape, then stripping her out of those sedate clothes.

He'd approached her, as he often had, but as usual she'd been all business without a single flirting note in her voice. Now, of course, he realized it was her professionalism and her awareness of students nearby that had kept her from engaging in anything other than respectful small talk.

One memory always led to another, and he realized…he'd been a fool. Always, in so many different ways, Issy had shown herself to be very special. He should have been more attuned to his own attraction and stated his interest instead of expecting her to act first.

Maybe he was too damned used to women chasing him.

Issy would never chase—except she had come up with a pretty creative way to get his attention…with the help of his meddling cousin.

And thinking of Amber, he knew he needed to clue her in on his and Issy's new relationship, especially after he pulled up to her house and for the third day in a row, found other men already there.

Issy stood on the porch, dressed casually in a T-shirt and shorts and looking sexier than ever with her dark red hair loose. By her animated face and hand gestures, Adam knew she was making her excuses, but the guys kept grinning and trying to persuade her otherwise.

Deciding to lend a hand, he slammed his door—and drew all their attention. He smiled as he made his way toward them.

"Adam," Issy said, sounding suddenly breathless. "You're early."

"I finished up sooner than I thought." He ignored Ken and Gary, stepped past them, scooped Issy in for a passionate kiss, and while she was preoccupied with that, he stepped them both inside and kicked the door shut. Ending the kiss with reluctance, he looked down at Issy's closed eyes and parted lips and appreciated the heavier way she breathed. "They'll leave now," he assured her.

Her heavy eyelids lifted. "Who?"

Ah, nice that the chemistry was so strong for both of them. "The yahoos on your porch."

"My porch," she repeated, and a second later her eyes flared. "The men!" She pushed Adam aside, opened the door and…

Damn, they both still stood there.

"I am *so* sorry," Issy said. She frowned at Adam to ensure they all knew where she placed the blame.

Ken grinned at her. "No problem."

Rubbing the smile off his mouth, Gary said, "Say yes, and we can get out of your way."

Aggressive confusion had Adam crossing his arms and mean-mugging both men.

"Adam," Issy said, "Ken and Gary are here about a game-day fundraiser."

"We have it on good authority that she's a shark at horseshoes." Ken gave her a sappy smile. "We need her on our team."

"I'm really not," Issy insisted. "I keep telling you—"

"Turly already told us." Gary slanted a look at Adam. "He said she's *real* good."

"So we *need* you," Ken repeated.

And damn it, Adam just knew they were wording their pleas in a way to annoy him.

"The fundraiser isn't for another month." He and his family always participated. Several different sports and games were set up and throughout the day fellow citizens competed for a fee. Whoever won each sport got to designate which local non-profit received the funds.

"Got to grab her up quick," Ken said, "before someone else does."

"If we win," Gary added, "the money will go to the town library."

Of all the underhanded tricks! Gary and Ken usually put their winnings toward the lake, adding benches for sitting, or trees along the shoreline to help draw carp.

The bait worked though, and Issy perked up. "Really? Oh, that's wonderful."

Fast, before he got pushed aside, Adam said, "I wanted you on my team—for horseshoes and volleyball. I figured we'd divide our wins with one going to the library, and the other to help with the feral cat population."

Even more enthused, she said, "Oh, Adam, that would be *perfect*!"

Adam reeled her on in, saying, "We could maybe try our hands at softball, too, if you're interested. Think of all the money we could donate if we won all three."

She grabbed him for a tight hug. Over her head, Adam let Gary and Ken see his smug satisfaction.

Because they were going out to dinner, where Adam could show the whole town that they were a couple, Issy said her goodbyes to the others and hurried inside for her purse.

Taking advantage of the moment, Adam propped a shoulder against the doorjamb and tried to make a point. “I’m glad to know you were only here to ask her to compete.”

Gary cocked a brow. “First I asked her out, and when she said no to that, I moved on to the games.”

Damn it. Provoked, Adam slowly straightened.

“Same here,” Ken said, drawing Adam’s frown his way. “I figured when I pulled up and heard her refusing Gary, I might have a chance. But I struck out, too.”

Of all the… Thumb to his chest, Adam stated, “Neither of you has a chance because she’s with *me*.”

“Sure, sure.” Clapping him on the shoulder, Ken turned to go. “Good luck convincing everyone else.”

“Just so you know,” Gary added, “I’ve been after her for a long time.”

Adam ground his teeth. “Now you can stop.”

“Maybe. Think I’ll wait and see how it works out with you first.” He saluted Adam and left to catch up with Ken.

Adam was still stewing when he felt a brush against his legs and looked down to find Cupid staring after the men. Adam knew if he went to pick up the cat, she’d shy away.

She was still pretty timid with most people. He could pet her with an outstretched arm, but she wasn’t keen on being held. Yet. He could force the issue, but would rather wait.

Between him, Issy, and his dad, Cupid was warming up. All she needed was plenty of love and patience. Issy had a wealth of both. “You should learn to be a guard cat. Keep all those other rats away.”

Cupid meowed, then darted in to find Issy.

He and the cat had something in common.

They were both crazy about Isabella Presley.

EVERY DAY FOR the rest of the week, Adam finished his day by showing up at Isabella's. They'd have dinner, make love, then sleep curled together.

The situation would have been perfect, except that far too often when he got to her place, he found other guys there. Oh, they had a variety of reasons for visiting that on the surface sounded innocent enough.

But he wasn't buying it.

Now that Issy was on the market, it seemed every bachelor in Buckhorn wanted to try his chances with her.

It got to where his routine included thinking about Issy when he wasn't with her, finally getting to her only to have to chase off the competition, and then spending the rest of his time trying to ensure she wasn't interested in other guys.

She helped by repeatedly stating her love. He'd gotten used to that, to hearing those three small but awesome words from her. Even though he hadn't yet said them back, he knew the truth.

He loved being with her, loved touching her, talking to her—and especially loved sex with her. He couldn't imagine a woman more compatible with him, and didn't even want to imagine himself with anyone else.

Isabella was it for him.

The only reason he hesitated to state his feelings was because it almost felt forced. Not by Isabella, but by his damned cousin who, he felt sure, was the one repeatedly tossing guys at her. Amber would probably do it to both annoy him and prod him toward declarations. But he wanted Issy to know he wasn't coerced in any way, to understand that he'd already been interested long before they ramped up things at the carnival. Kissing her had sealed the deal. Getting close to her had completely stolen his heart.

Given a little time, he could show her how much he cared, instead of merely telling her. But time didn't seem to be on his side.

Within an hour of them getting to the family picnic on Sunday, two local guys who'd showed up with Garrett began to flirt with her. Cupid wasn't happy about being in a carrier, and she especially didn't like the guys talking so loud.

They'd brought her along because Jordan wanted to check her over again. His uncle often did vet checks of the family pets at big gatherings. Eventually Cupid would come to enjoy all the attention, but for now, there'd be a quiet place in the house for her during their visit.

Using the cat as an excuse, Adam pointed the pushy guys in the direction of his Uncle Gabe's daughters, Briana, April and Kady. For sure, those three flirts would keep them occupied.

He glared at Garrett, who just grinned and hugged Zoey closer. "Problem, Adam?"

"No." Not since he got the guys to move on. If he had his way, he'd end the date-parade today. He said to Issy, "Cupid would probably like to get out of this carrier, and I'm betting Garrett and Zoey would love to meet her."

Garrett, who'd started to move toward one of the coolers for a beer, froze. He glanced at Adam, cocked a brow, and then proved himself loyal by saying, "Yeah, that'd be great. But why don't we all go inside first, in case Cupid freaks out?"

Issy, who'd been cooing to the cat, smiled at Garrett. "She's really very sweet—"

A feral snarl emerged.

Taking the carrier from Issy, Garrett soothed both the cat and her by saying, "Poor baby isn't liking all the commotion. Let's take her in." Winking at Adam, he added, "You can go ahead and have that talk with Amber. We'll be fine."

Zoey laughed. "My money's on Amber." She hooked her arm through Isabella's and got them moving.

"I'll be right back," Adam called after them.

Always happy to brag about her pet, Isabella nodded and off she went with his bemused cousin Garrett, and Zoey, who was always enthusiastic about everything.

It required only a short search before Adam located Amber in the kitchen, stealing a kiss from Noel Poet.

"Ahem," he said loudly.

Noel ignored him, but Amber jumped away guiltily. "Adam. Hey, you're here. What's up?"

Rolling his eyes, Noel said, "Judging by the look on his face, your goose is cooked, that's what."

"I don't know what you—"

Noel kissed her again, short and sweet. "I'll give you two some privacy."

"Traitor," Amber grumbled, then she pasted on a smile. "Adam. You do look a little grouchy. Everything going okay?"

Knowing Issy was in the house and could show up at any minute, Adam crowded close to whisper, "I thought you loved me."

She grinned. "I do. Very much."

"Then quit with the interfering."

On a feigned gasp of indignation, she said, "I *assist*. There's a difference."

"Your brand of assistance is about to make me insane."

Going serious, she said, "Hey, I called them off."

"Right." If that was true, she must not have been very convincing.

"I did," she insisted.

"When?"

"Soon as you told me you were involved, that day at her house." She shrugged. "I guess now that they've made note of her, they're free agents. Not my doing. Just men going after what they want."

"Issy?"

She patted Adam's shoulder. "You have to admit, the woman is a catch."

"Of course she is. She's beautiful and smart and sweet."

"Sexy, too?" Amber asked.

"Smokin' hot." He let out a breath. If it wasn't Amber encouraging the men, he needed to think of a way to *discourage* them.

"She's good with kids, too."

"You don't have to tell me." Adam rubbed the back of his neck. "She's incredible with them. Understanding and genuinely caring. One day, she'll make a terrific mother."

Both brows up, Amber asked, "With you as the father?"

"That's the plan, if I can—"

Behind him, Issy gasped.

Adam jerked around, and there she stood, Cupid cuddled in her arms, her eyes wide with astonishment.

Zoey and Garrett grinned behind her.

Damn it. Of all the ways he'd considered declaring himself, this wasn't one of them. "Hey."

She blinked those big blue eyes at him. "Hey."

Amber sighed. "I love it when a plan comes together." She bestowed an approving smile on each of them, gathered up Garrett and Zoey, and exited the kitchen.

For once, Adam appreciated her efforts. At least now he and Issy had some privacy.

He closed the distance between them, brushed his knuckles along her jaw, and asked, "What do you think?"

Face going pink, she whispered, "About?"

"Having babies with me. Not just yet, but someday. After we're married, of course."

For one heart-stopping moment, her bottom lip trembled. "I guess that depends." After a deep breath, she asked, "Do you love me?"

"Very, very much."

All the starch left her, and she even lightly punched him. "Why didn't you tell me?"

"I didn't want you to think it was Amber's idea. I know how she manipulates things."

"She does?"

How could Issy be unaware of that? "She told you not to tell me how you felt, right?"

Warily, Issy nodded. "Yes."

To let her know it was okay, Adam kissed her forehead. "Amber didn't want me to get too cocky about things." Without making an issue of it, he led her out of the kitchen and down the hall. He needed to ensure they'd have a few minutes alone, and he wanted to hold her—which meant getting her to an enclosed room where she could put down Cupid. "But after you gave me the cold shoulder so many times, there wasn't much chance of that happening."

"I *never.*"

"Yeah, honey, you did."

Under her breath, she grumbled, "Well, how's a woman to know what you're thinkin'?"

"Usually if I talked to a woman, she'd chat back, flirt a little, open the door to more. But you were always all business and I guess I didn't want to get shot down."

"I wouldn't have," she said gently. "And I hesitated to be bolder with you for the same reason. You're Buckhorn's most wanted bachelor, and I'm just—"

"Amazing." Pausing in the hallway, he kissed her. "Wonderful." Another kiss. "And mine."

Leaning into him, she sighed. "Yes." Then she shook her head and laughed. "Yes to being yours. I don't know about the rest."

"You can take my word on it." So much time they'd wasted. Sometimes his cousin was a genius—not that he'd ever admit it to her. "Amber also told me you were a little wild," he teased.

"*Wild?*" Face hotter now, Issy didn't hesitate when he led her into an empty bedroom and closed the door. "That's ridiculous."

Not really. He had no idea how Amber had known, but when it came to sex—or at least, sex with him—Isabella was open, free, and totally uninhibited.

In other words, *perfect.*

But then, she was pretty much perfect in everything she did, whether it was running a middle school library, caring for kids in need, charming the masses, or making him insane with lust. "I assume Amber told me that to get me intrigued. Thing is, I was always intrigued. You need to know that."

Sitting on the side of the bed, Issy released a wiggling Cupid who wanted to sniff the room. Without the cat to hold, she laced her fingers together. "You hid it well."

"No, honey, you're just not great at picking up the signals. Too many times, I was all but panting for you."

"No," she said with fascinated disbelief.

Adam had no problem reassuring her. "Yup. But now that we're together, it doesn't matter."

"Because you love me?" She said it as if she couldn't quite bend her brain around it.

That was his fault. In trying to prove a point with Amber, he'd left Isabella uncertain.

"How could I not?" he asked. "Everything about you has always drawn me, but with my cousin putting her nose into things, we've now been able to talk in a more..." He fumbled for the right word.

"Intimate way?"

"Yes." He grinned, thinking of all the ways they'd been intimate. "That." Sitting beside her, Adam took her worried hands and held them. "Not for a second do I want you to think Amber talked me into anything. I've always wanted you, Issy, always liked you and been drawn to you. If you'd opened up more a year ago, we'd probably be married by now."

Her eyes went round.

It wasn't a quite a proposal, but more like a declaration of intent.

"We have time," he told her. "Time to do everything you want, time for me to show you how much I care, time to just enjoy being together before we start rushing into new plans." He didn't want her to feel pressured.

Cupid wound around their legs, leaving her long tail out until she'd formed a furry shackle.

Carefully, so he wouldn't spook her, Adam scooped her up and into Issy's lap. "What do you say we start by getting engaged? That way everyone will know you're not available. We can take our time figuring out everything else."

She didn't even blink. "I'd like that."

Smiling, he said, "We can pick out rings whenever you want."

Nodding hard, she gasped, "Okay."

Adam had to kiss her, so he did. As usual, she tasted so good, stirred him on so many levels, that he got carried away. Things might have gotten inappropriate, given they were in his uncle's house, except that Cupid's tail hit him in the chin, reminding him of the here and now.

He leaned away with a grin. "I want everyone to know you're taken."

Staring at his mouth, she whispered, "Long as they know you're taken, too."

"I'll be telling it to everyone who'll listen." And definitely to anyone male who came sniffing around Issy.

"I love you," she whispered.

Adam cupped her face, his heart full. "I love you, too."

A tap sounded at the door, and Amber gave a loud, "Ahem."

Adam groaned. "What now?"

"Everyone's gathered to eat if you two want to make any—hint, hint—announcements."

Adam stood and opened the door. "It's uncanny how you do that."

Beaming, she bragged, "I have my skills."

Issy appeared at his side, leaning into him while holding Cupid. "Do your skills include ropin' in Noel Poet?"

Amber frowned. "I'm working on it."

From behind her, Noel said, "Good to know."

Aghast, Amber went still, then red in the face before slowly pivoting to face Noel. "It's rude to sneak up on people."

"That's never stopped you."

Adam enjoyed seeing his cousin in the hot seat for once.

Issy broke the growing tension with a happy laugh. "Neither of you are showin' Amber the appreciation she deserves." Issy smiled up at him. "Adam and I are gettin' engaged, and I couldn't be happier!"

"And before your head gets any bigger," Adam said to Amber, "you only played the *smallest* of roles in it."

"Small, but integral," Amber countered, grabbing them both for hugs. "Now let's go make that announcement!"

Noel caught her arm before she could take a single step away. "Since you already know what's going on, you don't need to be there." Ignoring her protests, he urged her into the room they'd just vacated, and right before he closed the door, he said to Adam, "Congrats to you both."

Surprised, Adam stared at the closed door, and slowly smiled.

"She deserves to be happy," Issy whispered.

They both heard Amber say, "Now wait just a—" Then her voice faded into a soft hum.

"She does," Adam agreed. "I'd say Noel has her well on her way." Putting a hand to the small of Issy's back, he led her out front. The sooner everyone knew Isabella's changed circumstances, the sooner he could relax.

And then they could get started on their future.

* * * * *

The Buckhorn Brothers—hot, protective,
and oh-so-alpha...especially around
the women they love.

Don't miss any of the Buckhorn series,
Available now from Lori Foster and HQN Books!
BUCKHORN BEGINNINGS
(featuring Sawyer and Morgan)

FOREVER BUCKHORN
(featuring Gabe and Jordan)

THE BUCKHORN LEGACY
(featuring Casey)

BUCKHORN EVER AFTER
(Shohn and Nadine's story)

BACK TO BUCKHORN
(Garrett and Zoey's story)

A BUCKHORN SUMMER
(Lisa and Gray's story)